The Stranger Waiting At The Altar Turned To Look At Her.

There was power in him, and a delicious sensuality that called to Ariana. By the time she joined him, she was feeling a sizzle of awareness that she fought to conceal.

Time seemed to catch its breath, and the ceremony passed in a haze. Finally, the moment came to recite their vows and exchange rings, and Lazzaro took her hand.

And that was when it happened.

When skin touched skin, the shock hit with such force that if Lazzaro hadn't been holding on to her, she'd have fallen. She glanced up to see his look of stunned disbelief. It seemed she wasn't the only one who'd felt it.

"What the hell was that?" he muttered, his mouth close to hers.

"Not quite the first words I'd hoped to hear my husband speak," she whispered back, "but an excellent question. What just happened…?"

Dear Reader,

I never thought I could love anyone as much—or more—than my family...until I met my husband. And then I was certain I couldn't love another as deeply or with such commitment, until I had my son.

I've always found parenthood to be an almost indescribable experience. The feelings are so intense. One minute you couldn't be happier, the next you're overcome with exhaustion. You're stuffed full of determination to do the right thing for this precious, vulnerable creature. To strive to make their life the best possible. It's like being on an emotional roller coaster with an underlying joy providing the tracks beneath the careening wheels. I have to laugh when I think of how children pull every possible emotion out of you...for better or worse.

I was thinking about this one day, about how being a parent forces you to examine everything about yourself and your life in order to decide...is this how I want to raise my child? Should I do this for my son...or that? That question was the springboard for this story, a story about a parent so determined to protect his son that he drafted a marital contract to ensure his son found love.

I thoroughly enjoyed writing this particular book. This story also marks the last in THE DANTE LEGACY series. I can't tell you how sad it makes me to walk away from this very special family. Of course...there are four Dante cousins. If you'd be interested in my writing their stories at some point in the future, don't hesitate to let me know at Day@DayLeclaire.com.

Enjoy!

Day Leclaire

DAY
LECLAIRE

DANTE'S CONTRACT
MARRIAGE

Published by Silhouette Books
America's Publisher of Contemporary Romance

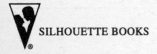

SILHOUETTE BOOKS

®

ISBN-13: 978-0-373-76899-8
ISBN-10:   0-373-76899-0

DANTE'S CONTRACT MARRIAGE

Visit Silhouette Books at www.eHarlequin.com

Printed in U.S.A.

DAY LECLAIRE

USA TODAY bestselling author Day Leclaire lives and works in the perfect setting—on an island off the North Carolina coast. Living in an environment where she can connect with primal elements that meld the moodiness of an ever-changing ocean, unfettered wetlands teeming with every creature imaginable, and the ferocity of both hurricanes and nor'easters that batter the fragile island, she's discovered the perfect setting for writing passionate books that offer a unique combination of humor, emotion and unforgettable characters.

Described by Harlequin as "one of our most popular writers ever!", Day's tremendous worldwide popularity has made her a member of Harlequin's prestigious "Five Star Club," with sales totaling more than five million books. She is a three-time winner of both The Colorado Award of Excellence and The Golden Quill Award. She's won *Romantic Times BOOKreviews* magazine's Career Achievement Award and Love and Laughter Award, a Holt Medallion, a Booksellers' Best Award, and has received an impressive ten nominations for the prestigious Romance Writers of America RITA® Award.

Day's romances touch the heart and make you care about her characters as much as she does. In Day's own words, "I adore writing romances, and can't think of a better way to spend each day." For more information, visit Day on her Web site at www.dayleclaire.com.

To Nancy Cecelia Totton.
You've been missed for far too long.

Prologue

"Cut it out, Ariana." Lazzaro Dante glared at the pesky five-year-old. "I don't like it when you do that."

"But I can zap you," she protested. "And I don't even have to rub my socks on the carpet first. See?"

She proved it by poking him again. A faint sizzle rippled along his arm, one that caused all the hairs to stand up on end. He jerked back from her and rubbed the spot. "I said cut it out."

Hurt blossomed in chocolate-brown eyes that seemed to fill half her face. "I'm just playing. Don't you want to play with me?"

Was she nuts? Of course he didn't want to play with her. He was twelve, nearly a teenager. She was little more than a baby. "Go ask Marco. He likes those kinds of games."

She pouted. "It's not the same. I can't shock him. I tried already. I can only shock you."

"Well, I don't like it."

Her dark brows drew together in a worried frown. "Does it hurt?"

"No." And it didn't. He just felt uncomfortable, like ants were racing beneath his skin and making him itchy and jumpy and confused, all at the same time. But maybe if he claimed it hurt, she'd stop touching him. "A little, okay? So don't do it anymore."

Contrition swept across her face. Heck, she even looked as if she might cry, which filled him with a pang of guilt. Having grown up with brothers and male cousins—with the exception of Gianna, who acted as though she were one of the guys—he wasn't used to dealing with girls. If you weren't happy with something a brother or cousin did, you just slugged them until they stopped. But he didn't dare treat Ariana that way.

He regarded her uneasily. For one thing, she was tiny and looked as if she might break if he stepped wrong. And some idiot had dressed her in a pink dress covered in bows with layers of petticoats. She even wore little lace socks with her shiny black shoes. How did you play in that sort of getup? In fact, now that he thought about it, she looked more like a doll than a girl. Somebody ought to stick her on a shelf someplace where she wouldn't get hurt.

"Ariana, come here, please."

Lazz sighed in relief at the sound of Vittorio Romano's voice. Good. Her dad would take care of her now, put her away so she wouldn't get dirty or broken. He waited until she'd been lifted into her father's arms before making good his escape. Tossing aside his book of logic puzzles, he joined his brothers. Maybe if he hung around his twin, Marco, she'd get them mixed up and bug his brother instead of him.

Ariana wrapped her arms around her father's neck and buried her face against his shoulder. "He doesn't like me," she said. "Fix it, Papa."

Vittorio chuckled, shooting a swift grin toward Dominic Dante, surprised when his friend didn't share his amusement. "You want me to make Lazz like you?"

"Yes."

"I'm sorry, *bambolina,* it doesn't work that way." He signaled for his daughter's nanny. "Go with Rosa now. She'll play with you. Or you can ask Grandmother Penelope to read you your favorite Mrs. Pennywinkle book. She's in the garden painting or writing."

Ariana didn't protest. She struggled to master her tears before giving her father a dutiful kiss on the cheek. With a final forlorn glance in Lazz's direction, she took Rosa's hand and trotted off.

Vittorio turned to Dominic, stiffening at his friend's expression. "What's wrong? You look quite ill. Can I get you something?"

Dominic shook his head. "No, no. There's nothing you can get me. Damn it to hell. It's The Inferno," he murmured. "My God. It may not be how it's experienced as adults, but I'll bet every last fire diamond the Dantes possess that we just witnessed the beginnings of The Inferno."

"You mean that silly zapping game? Don't be ridiculous, Dom. Ariana is still a baby and Lazz a boy." Vittorio hesitated, striving for delicacy. "I know you said something about The Inferno in passing when we were in college, but—"

A reminiscent smile flickered across Dominic's face before fading to grimness. "I believe we were blind drunk at the time or I'd never have mentioned it. We don't speak of it, except with other Dantes. I'm surprised you remember."

"The concept of The Inferno is a bit hard to forget," Vittorio said drily. He tilted his head to one side. "But surely you don't believe it? You claimed it was nothing more than a Dante family myth."

"It's no myth, despite what I told you. I felt it myself not many years later."

Vittorio smiled. "I believe that's called love, though some call it lust. Or infatuation. A lightning bolt from heaven…or as it eventually turns out, from hell." He slapped Dominic on the back. "Your family has simply chosen a more clever name for it. But everyone has those romantic stirrings toward their wife."

"It wasn't with Laura," Dominic instantly denied. "I decided to ignore what I felt toward the woman The Inferno chose for me and married for business reasons. As it turns out, my life and marriage have been nothing short of a disaster."

Vittorio stared, shocked. "Surely not."

"My father warned me. He said I'd regret it if I didn't marry where The Inferno struck. I didn't listen."

"It was Primo who put those ideas in your head in the first place," Vittorio argued. "Of course he'd warn you."

"You still don't understand." Dominic spun to confront his friend, his eyes black with a combination of pain and fierce determination. "I didn't listen to The

Inferno, and I've been cursed ever since. I can't allow that to happen to my children. I'll do whatever it takes to make certain they don't suffer my fate."

"I don't like the sound of this."

"I'm not proposing anything that hasn't been done for centuries." Dominic spoke fast and low, with a worrisome underlying urgency. "I want to betroth our children. Draw up a contract to that effect."

"Don't be ridiculous." Vittorio allowed a hint of sharpness to color his words. "Even if I were to consider it, we couldn't force our children to honor such an outrage, not if they were unwilling."

"If I'm right, we won't need to force them. The first time they touch as adults they'll be bonded. They'll be only too happy to marry. And even if there's an initial reluctance, they'll change their minds after a few months of wedded bliss. All we have to do is get them in front of a priest."

Vittorio shook his head. He couldn't believe he was listening to this insane scheme. "And how do you propose we get them to the altar?"

"Like I said. We offer an incentive to sweeten the deal." He hesitated and lowered his voice to a mere whisper. "Have you heard of Brimstone?"

Vittorio stiffened at the mention of the infamous fire diamond. "I've always wondered if it were real or another Dante legend."

A small smile played around Dominic's mouth. "It's real enough."

"I've heard the diamond carries a curse."

"Or a blessing. It depends on your perspective."

"And your perspective is?"

"That it's up to the individual person and how he or she chooses to use the diamond."

"And how do you intend to use it?"

Dominic's smile grew. "Now that my father has given me control of our family business, I also have control of Brimstone. I propose that we make the diamond part of the contract. We'll put the stone in a bank deposit box for safekeeping. If Lazzaro and Ariana marry by the time your daughter turns twenty-five, the diamond will be split between the two families."

"Literally?" Vittorio asked, intrigued.

Dominic shook his head. "No, that would be very bad luck. Dantes will pay you half the worth of the diamond."

"And if the two refuse to marry?"

A fevered expression glittered in Dominic's eyes. "Then Brimstone will be sacrificed, thrown into the deepest part of the ocean."

"You've lost your mind."

Dominic laughed. "My soul, perhaps, but not my mind."

Vittorio hesitated, weighing the pros and cons despite himself. "The truly frightening part of this is that I'm actually considering your offer." The distinctive squeak of a wheelchair came from nearby and Vittorio glanced over his shoulder to make certain his mother-in-law wasn't close enough to overhear. There would be hell to pay if she caught wind of this.

"I'm hoping you'll do more than consider it," Dominic replied. "I'm hoping you'll agree."

"I can't believe I'm saying this, but I agree to your proposal."

A hint of contentment settled on Dominic's face. For the first time since the Dantes had arrived in Italy, Vittorio realized just how stressed his friend had become over the past few years. It saddened him to see Dom change from the charming, carefree schoolboy he'd once known to this hardened businessman. It also filled him with a vague unease. Maybe there was something to his story. Maybe the Dantes were cursed. Perhaps the fates had chosen to balance the Dantes' astonishing good fortune in the business world with a cursed personal life.

Vittorio crossed himself surreptitiously. "I want to make it clear, Dom. I refuse to force Ariana to the altar if she chooses not to marry."

"She'll marry Lazz. They both will agree to it, if only to keep a priceless diamond from being destroyed." He shot Vittorio a confident look. "If I'm right and that spark between children grows to an Inferno between adults, you'll benefit financially while I'll have the greatest gift of all."

"And what's that?"

Dominic stared at where his sons were heaped in a pile with Vittorio's son, Constantine. They formed a squirming mass of arms and legs, heads and tails. Their laughter rang out, the sound more precious than anything else in his life. "I'll have gained peace of mind."

One

From: Lazzaro_Dante@DantesJewelry.com
Date: 2008, August 04 08:02 PDST
To: Bambolina@fornitore.it
Subject: Marriage Contract, Premarital Conditions
Ariana, as discussed in our recent phone conversation, I'm sending my first marital condition.
Condition #1: Absolutely, positively, unequivocally **no secrets**.

August 7, 2008

"I hate secrets."

Lazzaro Dante made the statement so emphatically that it caused Ariana Romano to fall silent. Honesty compelled him to admit to himself that he hated secrets almost as much as he hated The Inferno—a myth his family considered a reality. The Inferno, or rather what his brothers and their wives perceived as some nebulous and fiery connection between soul mates that struck at first touch, had recently formed an exclusive club to which all his family members belonged, except him. As far as he was concerned, the family "curse" didn't exist, and nothing anyone could say or do would change his mind. Ever.

He could hear his fiancée's breath catch through the phone line and sensed her searching for an appropriate reply to his pronouncement. "I realize we've never met, but you are aware you're marrying a woman, yes?" she asked. "Secrets and women go together like handbags and heels."

Her comment caught him off guard. Perhaps it was the way she said it, with a hint of gentle humor sweeping through her odd accent. Her English, which she'd acquired from her British grandmother, carried the upper-crust echo of tea and crumpets and combined with the sunny warmth of her native tongue, an Italian lilt that orchestrated her every word.

"And you do realize I'm not Marco, right?" he reminded her.

"Your brother has explained as much," she replied with far too much equanimity. "He's visited us many times on Dantes business and says that despite being twins, the two of you are as different as night and day."

"True."

"For instance…he's charming and you are not."

Lazz straightened in his chair. "I'm logical."

"He is amusing. You…not so much. I believe that is the way Marco puts it."

"When I see my brother, I'll be sure to explain precisely where he can put it."

If she heard the muttered comment, she didn't respond to it. "Marco is also handsome and intelligent and kind. Not to mention an excellent kisser." A pregnant pause followed the pronouncement. "Should I expect my future husband to be none of those things?"

He locked on to the most vital portion of her comment. An irrational anger exploded in him, an emotion far out of proportion to the situation. *Not again,* an insidious voice whispered. No way would he share another woman with his brother, especially not someone he planned to marry.

He'd been through that with Caitlyn, a woman he'd been on the verge of proposing to, when Marco had tricked her into marriage by posing as Lazz. He wouldn't—*couldn't*—marry Ariana if she expected him to be a stand-in for Marco. Logic be damned, he flat-out refused to be a substitute for any man.

"You and Marco kissed?"

She must have heard the edge in his voice, because she answered promptly. "Before he met Caitlyn, yes. But it didn't rock either of our worlds." Her use of the idiom would have amused him if the circumstances had been different. "Despite his expertise, it was like kissing in the hopes of finding a lover and finding only a good friend. Do you know what I mean?"

"No."

"Ah, well. Perhaps it's never happened to you." Again came that tiny pause, and he had the strong sus-

picion she was laughing at him. "Are you…inexperi-
enced?"

"Hell, no!"

"I thought since you've been so insistent that you're
Marco's complete opposite that perhaps this is another
area in which you are lacking."

She was poking at him, the same as when she'd been
a child, he realized with equal parts amusement and annoyance. "You're playing a dangerous game," he warned.
"Jerk a kitten's tail, and Marco might scratch you. Jerk
my tail, and you're dealing with an entirely different
kind of animal."

Her breath escaped in a soft laugh. "Touché. I have
gathered as much from our negotiations. Your list of
marital demands have been quite…interesting."

"As have yours. Particularly your latest, which is why
I'm calling." Lazz regarded the printout he held with a
basic masculine confusion. "Why do you want your own
room? I can understand your own bedroom, but—"

"I require a room with a lock and a guarantee of
utter privacy. Did I phrase my request in a way that
confused you?"

"Not at all." Suspicion roared to the surface. "You
phrased it in a way that makes me wonder what you're
hiding and why."

"I am not hiding anything. I'm being quite explicit.
This is not a matter for one of your infamous negotiations. Refuse my request and it's a deal-breaker."

"Why?" he repeated.

Her laugh came to him, rich and earthy, and filled
with a honeyed warmth. "How many times must I tell
you? I'm a woman. Women need their privacy."

"Your own bedroom isn't private enough?"

"I can't do what I have in mind in a bedroom."

"That's a relief," he muttered.

Ariana's laughter teased him again, decimating the barriers of logic and rational thought Lazz had worked so hard to erect. He struggled to remember what she looked like, but nothing came to him, possibly because nearly two full decades had passed since he'd last seen her. Maybe he'd ask Marco. His brother had conducted protracted business dealings with the Romano family. Worse, Ariana and Marco had kissed. No question he would be able to describe Ariana. Knowing Marco, he'd be able to do it right down to the last tiny freckle.

Lazz grimaced. Or perhaps he wouldn't ask his brother a damn thing, since he suspected Marco would use the opportunity to either give him some serious grief, or even worse, try and talk him out of honoring the contract their father had signed with Vittorio Romano. And all because of that ridiculous Inferno nonsense.

"Are you going to tell me why you need a private room?" Lazz asked again.

"No."

"You simply expect me to comply with no explanation or clarification?"

"Yes. I expect you to comply the same way you expect me to comply with your marital demands." She paused, before asking delicately, "How many are we up to now? Ten?"

"Five," he corrected. "Six, if you count the one I'm sending you later today about the disposition of Brimstone."

"Of course that one counts. And how many have I made?"

"Three."

"Which leaves me with three to spare, should I choose to use them. And maybe I will. Maybe I'll save my extra three demands for after we're married. You can be the genie to my wishes." Her sigh of pleasure drifted across continents. "I quite like that idea."

For some reason that sigh caused a hunger to gnaw at the pit of his stomach. "That's not how it works."

"It works however we say it does. You claim you're the logical one."

"I *am* the logical one." He always had been, and marriage to Ariana wouldn't change that fact, a point he intended to make crystal clear. He attempted to get them back on topic. "About the room. If you'd just explain—"

"Are you worried that I intend to take a lover? Would you feel better about my request if I tell you I promise to honor my vow to remain faithful to you for the duration of our marriage?"

Yes. He closed his eyes at the silent acknowledgment. He knew where his suspicions came from. Understood his knee-jerk reaction to anything that hinted at a secret or a hidden agenda. He could lay that little issue squarely at Marco's door—and at his own. Just as Marco had used subterfuge to sweep in and carry Caitlyn away, Lazz had been every bit as guilty of a few secrets and deceptions of his own in the course of that entire debacle. Still, it had been quite a blow to his pride when the woman he'd hoped to marry had chosen his twin brother over him.

The entire incident had left a sour taste in Lazz's mouth and created a general distaste for lies and deception. And yet, here he was embroiled in just that. It might have been of his father's making, but he'd chosen to keep the reasons for his impending marriage a secret from two of the people he loved most in his life. And though he attempted to rationalize his decision, there were certain lines that couldn't be smudged.

What he was doing was wrong and he knew it.

"You're not going to tell me why you need a private room, are you?" Lazz asked. "Despite my condition that we not have secrets from each other, you still refuse to explain."

"I'm sorry, Marco."

"Lazz," he corrected softly.

"Now I really am sorry." There was no mistaking her sincerity. "I swear I wasn't 'jerking your tail' as you called it. Using your brother's name was an honest mistake. You sound so much like him."

"I look like him, too," Lazz warned. "But I'd appreciate it if you'd remember my name by the time we marry. My grandparents might find it a bit suspicious if you keep calling me Marco. They believe we met and fell in love the last time you were in San Francisco, and it's imperative that they continue to believe that for the duration of our marriage."

"Of course. You made it a condition, one I heartily approve of." A note of formality stole the summer warmth from her voice. "I will be very careful to play my part. Believe me, I don't wish my grandmother or my mother to find out about this devil's contract any more than you want your grandparents to discover the truth."

"My grandparents would do everything in their power to stop the wedding if they knew about the contract." Primo had once told him that to marry without The Inferno would turn a blessing into a curse. So Lazz had allowed his grandparents to believe that he and Ariana had experienced what he privately denied.

"Don't you find it disturbing that you're marrying a virtual stranger," she asked, "knowing nothing about what sort of person I am?"

"It's not forever, Ariana. And it enables us to achieve the same goal. We both want to prevent Brimstone from being thrown away."

"So we marry for profit."

Her concern came through loud and clear. She sounded on the verge of backing out, something he couldn't allow to happen. "If privacy is what you need in order to make all of this more palatable for you, you can have it. I agree to your third condition. I also promise we won't stay married a minute longer than necessary."

"How can I possibly refuse such a romantic offer?" she asked lightly.

His grin slid into his voice. "I can't imagine. So, when are you coming over?"

"Not until right before the ceremony. Both my grandmother and mother are shrewd women. I'm afraid if they see us together, they won't believe our story of a whirlwind love affair. It took a lot of maneuvering to convince my mother to delay our arrival. She wanted to fly over weeks beforehand. Fortunately, once I explained my problem to my father, he supported my request. We arrive the morning of the rehearsal."

"That makes sense." Lazz glanced at the calendar on his desk. "Not long now. Just three more weeks."

"August 28th. And then we'll be married," she murmured.

"Temporarily." Lazz's mouth tightened. And The Inferno be damned.

"So what's his latest demand?" Constantine asked his sister. Ever since the contract between their father and Dominic Dante had come to light, her brother had scoured the fine print, watching over the negotiations like a hawk.

"He's just reiterating one of his older ones. We're to have no secrets."

Constantine grinned. "Are you serious?"

"No. But he is." She dropped into the chair in front of her brother's desk and lifted her feet to rest on the edge. "I'm beginning to realize that Lazz is nothing like Marco."

"I like Marco. He's fun."

"Maybe a little too much fun, just as his brother is a little too much business." She released her breath in a sigh. "Isn't there a happy medium?"

"You're looking at him."

Ariana chuckled and nudged a stack of files with her bare toe. They cascaded in his direction, creating a flurry of papers that swamped his desk. "Aren't we full of ourselves, especially for virtual paupers."

Constantine busied himself for a moment, straightening the papers she'd knocked over, but Ariana understood. They'd been broke for years due to a series of bad investments their father had made. Since then, they'd lived off their name, as well as off friends who were willing to pick up the tab in order to have the Romanos grace their homes. And though it didn't seem to bother their father, Ariana had watched with serious concern the impact it had on her brother.

Constantine hated being broke. Hated freeloading. Hated having their maternal grandmother, Penelope, use the money from her Mrs. Pennywinkle royalty checks to keep the Romano estate intact. He had a head for business, but so far lacked investors. And the few who'd shown interest didn't plan to allow Constantine to run the concern, but simply wanted the Romano name attached to the project and her brother installed as a figurehead.

This marriage offered salvation for all of them. With their share of Brimstone, it would be more than enough to seed Constantine's business, as well as provide her father with a comfortable retirement.

"Do you think Grandmother suspects anything?" Ariana asked.

"Not at all. She's downright giddy over your wedding."

"I'm so relieved she's well enough to come."

A light tap sounded at the door, and the object of their conversation wheeled herself through the doorway. "Oh, there you are." She beamed at her grandchildren. "I was hoping to find you here. I just wanted a word with Ariana about a few wedding details."

Constantine shoved back his chair. "In that case, I'll make myself scarce." He bent over his frail grandmother and kissed her rose-petal-soft cheek. "You call me if you need anything, Gran," he said before making good his escape.

"Would you like some tea?" Ariana asked. Even though Penelope had left England more than fifty years ago when she'd married her Italian-born husband, she still preferred a cup of hot tea over any other beverage.

"I just had some, thank you." She regarded Ariana with china-blue eyes that sparkled with good humor. "I have to confess, I told a small fib just now."

Ariana grinned. "You didn't want to discuss wedding plans? I'm shocked."

Penelope waved that aside. "You and my dear daughter are more than capable of handling the wedding arrangements on your own. Plus you have all of the Dantes at your disposal."

"So, if this isn't about my wedding…" Ariana tilted her head to one side in question.

"You know perfectly well what this is about."

Ariana blew out a sigh. "Mrs. Pennywinkle."

"Yes, Mrs. Pennywinkle. You can't delay any longer."

The stories her grandmother created were beautifully illustrated tales, all about a china doll named Nancy who passed from needy child to needy child. With each subsequent owner came exciting adventures and heartrending problems for whichever youngster came into possession of the doll. By the end of the book, Nancy had helped resolve the child's problems and magically moved on to the next boy or girl in need. Ariana even owned the very first Nancy doll to come off the production line. It was one of her most treasured possessions.

"Have you finished the sketches the publisher requested?"

"The portfolio's ready to go, as is the storyline,"

Ariana admitted. "But I'm not sure Talbot Publishing is ready for such a significant change to books that have become classics over the years."

"Nonsense."

Ariana curled deeper into her chair. "I'm serious. My artistic style is nothing like yours. I'm not certain children will take to the change."

"It's time the books were revamped. Mrs. Pennywinkle has been in serious need of a face-lift for years now." A tiny frown marred the beauty of Penelope's English rose complexion. "Sales are dropping. If I don't find a way to turn it around—" She broke off with a shrug.

Ariana froze, understanding dawning. "Your money... It's running out?"

"It will if we don't get Mrs. Pennywinkle turned around." She leaned forward, lines of worry furrowing her brow. "Your mother doesn't have the talent or the interest. But you do."

"I definitely have the interest. It hasn't been decided whether I have sufficient talent. Which reminds me..." Ariana hesitated, reluctant to broach the subject. "I asked Lazz for a room where I can work on my illustrations, and he's curious about why I need both the room and such privacy. Would you mind if I tell him about Mrs. Pennywinkle?"

"You mustn't," Penelope cut in, her agitation increasing. "The Dantes attract media attention the way bread attracts butter. It'll get out. People will discover I'm Mrs. Pennywinkle. It'll be like it was after my accident."

Compassion filled Ariana at the mention of the accident that had killed her grandfather and chained Penelope to a wheelchair for the rest of her life. And though she understood why her grandmother preferred to keep her identity private, and respected that decision, Ariana had also made a promise to Lazz. She closed her eyes. There was no question which promise took precedence. Her grandmother's well-being came before all else.

"If you prefer I not tell Lazz what I'm up to, of course I'll respect your wishes," she said gently. "Besides, there's nothing to tell him. Not until your publisher accepts me as the new Mrs. Pennywinkle."

Penelope relaxed ever so slightly. "Since I'm no longer capable of continuing the series, thanks to these arthritic hands of mine, he won't have any choice."

Ariana wasn't as certain. Profit was the bottom line in today's business world, and if Talbot Publishing didn't feel her talent could change the face of Mrs. Pennywinkle in a way that would enhance the bottom line, they'd find someone else or allow the series to end. She'd do just about anything to ensure that didn't happen.

She shot her grandmother a concerned glance. She could only hope it all worked out in the end…and that she could keep the truth from Lazz for the length of their temporary marriage. Besides, it was only one tiny secret. Perhaps he wouldn't mind.

"So, what's her latest demand?" Marco asked.

Lazz scanned the printout of Ariana's e-mail for the umpteenth time. "You're married. Explain this to me. What the hell does it mean when she says she needs a private room? One that I won't invade, no less. Why does she need an entire room in order to be private?"

"And more importantly, why can't you invade it?" Marco asked.

"Yes, exactly. I mean, no, damn it! I wouldn't invade. Much." Lazz winced at his brother's bark of laughter. "Does Caitlyn have a private room?"

"Of course. I call it the bathroom, but she's turned it into some sort of female sanctuary, and God forbid I enter at the wrong time."

"When's the wrong time?"

Marco grinned. "Anytime she's in there."

"You're joking around, and I'm asking a serious question here."

Marco held up his hands in surrender. "Caitlyn has private areas. All women have them. They need places they can go to be alone and enjoy their femininity with all the delightful mystery that entails."

Lazz crumpled the e-mail in his fist. "Apparently, Ariana needs an entire room in order to be feminine."

"If it's such a problem, maybe you should reconsider marrying her."

"So you've said." Lazz's voice cooled. "As has Nicolò, twice. And Sev, at least a half dozen times."

"They're worried about you." Marco attempted to placate. "We all are. You don't have to honor that damnable contract Dad drew up. And you sure as hell don't have to marry Ariana in order to get your hands on Brimstone. No diamond, no matter how valuable, is worth that sort of sacrifice. None of us expect it of you."

Lazz lifted an eyebrow. "I'm surprised you all

aren't worried about the curse if I don't go through with the marriage."

"That diamond is only cursed if we believe it is," Marco said with a hint of unease. "Sev has secured our position in the jewelry world. It's ridiculous to believe that without Brimstone our family will never know true happiness or success. That's just a silly fairy tale."

"Just like it's ridiculous to believe The Inferno is anything more than a silly fairy tale?" Lazz asked pointedly.

Marco's jaw took on a stubborn slant. "That's different. One legend has nothing to do with the other."

"Right."

"Oh, can the sarcasm, will you? You're making a mistake marrying Ariana for business reasons, and you know it."

"So Sev and Nicolò have said." Lazz lobbed the balled e-mail in the direction of the trash can. It bounced off the rim before landing in the basket. "They think it's a mistake to marry Ariana because she's not my Inferno bride."

"I happen to agree with them," Marco said with deceptive mildness.

"Fortunately for all of us, I don't believe in The Inferno or its curse."

"Blessing."

Lazz ignored the interruption. "Ariana and I have e-mailed extensively, and we both agree. We'll marry. We'll put on a show for our grandparents for a few months. And then we'll go our separate ways. At some point, we'll have the marriage terminated."

Marco shook his head in open disgust. "I'm surorised at Dad. Considering how miserable he and Mom were, why would he want to force you into a similar type of marriage?"

"How many times do I have to explain? This isn't a real marriage." Lazz fought to control his impatience with only limited success. "Ariana and I will fulfill the terms of the contract and then have a friendly parting of the ways. Brimstone will be saved, and we'll buy out the Romanos' share of the stone. Nothing could be simpler and, best of all, everyone wins."

"If you really believe it'll be that easy, you're crazy. Primo and Nonna think you're marrying because of The Inferno. You've gone out of your way to give them that impression. Now you're stuck maintaining the pretense for the duration of your marriage. The minute you and Ariana divorce, they'll realize the truth." Marco leaned in, his expression unusually grim. "When that happens, it's going to crush them."

"I don't want them hurt," Lazz admitted. "But better they think I was mistaken about The Inferno than they find out about Dad's contract. In my opinion, that would crush them more than my confusing lust for The Inferno."

"You're wrong. They'd be more hurt to discover you're marrying for any reason other than love."

After a moment's consideration, Lazz was forced to concede the accuracy of his brother's observation. "Then I convince them that Ariana and I were in love when we married and that it simply didn't work out. I thought it was The Inferno and it wasn't. A simple case of wishful thinking. My understanding is that Ariana's grandmother, Penelope, and mother, Caro-

lina, also believe it's a love match and we don't wan
to disabuse either of them of that notion. The fact tha
Ariana and I have only met by e-mail will remain ou
little secret."

"I'll be interested to see your reaction when you two
really meet."

"Why?" The question slipped out before Lazz could
prevent it.

Marco shook his head with a mocking smile. "I'l
just let you find out for yourself."

"You're not going to tell me anything, are you?"

"I'll tell you this much… She's gorgeous. Passion
ate about life and everything in it. Has a terrific sense
of humor. And she has a soft spot when it comes to
children."

"You forgot to mention that she's a good kisser."

Marco laughed. "Told you, did she? Yes, she's a
good kisser. So, when's the big meet and greet?"

"Ariana and her family are scheduled to come in the
day before the ceremony. We'll get together privately
right before the rehearsal."

Marco's amusement faded. "You're crazy if you
think one brief meeting is going to establish enough
of a rapport between you to convince everyone you
two are romantically involved. You know nothing
about each other and yet you think you can fake an intimate relationship—fake it well enough to convince
Primo and Nonna, as well as Ariana's mother and
grandmother, that the two of you are madly in love."

"Since it's only for one evening, plus the reception
after the wedding, I think we can pull it off, assuming
everyone keeps their collective mouths shut."

"Well, good luck. Primo and Nonna will be tough enough. But you're really going to need to watch your step with Penelope. She's a canny old bird. Too bad you don't have my charm."

"Fortunately, I have the brains you lack."

Marco stood. "One last question before I leave you to your facts and figures. Have you warned your bride-to-be about The Inferno yet?"

Lazz regarded his brother in genuine bewilderment. "Why would I want to do that?"

Marco frowned. "Didn't you tell me that one of the conditions of your marriage was that you won't have any secrets from each other?"

"Fairy tales are not secrets." With any luck at all, this was one fairy tale he'd never have cause to repeat.

"A word of warning. You may not consider it a secret, but Ariana may have a different view," Marco said in parting. "Women can be funny about the details."

Lazz groaned. Damn, but he didn't like the sound of that. He could only hope his brother's comment didn't prove to be as prophetic as it felt.

Two

From: Lazzaro_Dante@DantesJewelry.com
Date: 2008, August 04 23:28 PDST
To: Bambolina@fornitore.it
Subject: Marriage Contract, Premarital Conditions...
Addendum
Forgot to mention...I must request that my grand-parents be kept in the dark about the existence of the contract between my father and yours.
Condition #2: Maintain a convincing facade of ro-mantic bliss in the presence of my grandparents.
L.

From: Bambolina@fornitore.it
Date: 2008, August 05 09:17 CEST
To: Lazzaro_Dante@DantesJewelry.com

Subject: Re: Marriage Contract, Premarital Conditions...Addendum

Fine, fine. Both your conditions are acceptable. I would also like to keep the reason for our marriage from my mother, Carolina, and my grandmother, Penelope. Not a secret of course, since you don't believe in them. Just a little white lie (for which we will both go straight to hell). I have told them we met and fell madly, passionately in love on my last visit to San Francisco. Does that work for you?

Ciao! Ariana

August 28, 2008

The morning of her wedding, Ariana woke to a world encased in fog. She wandered out onto the balcony of her hotel room at Le Premier and felt as though she were stepping into a cloud. It blanketed her in cool droplets of moisture that sparkled like a thousand individual diamonds.

Carolina wandered out onto the balcony and handed her daughter a mug of fragrant coffee. "How did you sleep?" she asked with a yawn.

"Really well. Between our flight being delayed all those hours and the jet lag, I fell off the minute I crawled into bed."

"We should have flown in earlier," Carolina said. "I never should have let you talk us into flying in the day before the ceremony."

"I didn't consider the possibility we might get grounded due to weather," Ariana conceded. "And I should have."

Though privately she thought it couldn't have worked out any better if she'd planned it. Not only had they missed the rehearsal, but the rehearsal dinner, as well. Now she only had to face the wedding. Anything between now and then that seemed a bit off or odd would be put down to wedding jitters. After that, she and Lazz just needed to put on a loving front long enough to get through the reception, and they'd be in the clear.

"Will it stay foggy like this? I'd so hoped for sunshine."

"It'll burn off in time," Ariana reassured. She glanced past her mother toward her grandmother. "Come out and look at this. It's amazing."

Penelope wheeled herself onto the balcony. Ariana crouched to wrap an arm around her grandmother while Carolina clutched her other hand, three generations of women united. "It's so strange to think we won't be returning to Italy together," Carolina murmured. "In a few hours you'll be married and living in a strange country with a husband you barely know."

"When it's right, it's right," Ariana replied lightly.

There wasn't time for more chatter. With three women in one hotel suite, every second counted as they prepared for the wedding. Little by little, order gave way to confusion, which gave way to chaos, which gave way to emotion-diffusing drama. Tears were shed, then rinsed away, just as the summertime sunshine rinsed away the final wisps of fog. As the hours ticked by and the time approached for the Romanos to leave for the church, tension turned to laughter and bittersweet reminiscences. Chaos organized itself into mild confusion, which drifted toward a messy sort of order.

At long last, Ariana stood in the middle of the suite, garbed in a gown that all three women had unanimously chosen as their favorite. The pearl-white color complimented her complexion and made her eyes seem deeper and darker, while the fitted bodice drew attention to the trim figure she'd inherited from her mother. The skirt floated around her like the wisps of fog she'd been admiring earlier. And she wore a lace-and-tulle veil that had belonged to her great–grandmother, anchored in place by a fire diamond tiara delivered to their hotel suite only that morning—a wedding gift from Lazz.

Her mother fluttered around her, making final minute adjustments, while Penelope simply sat and beamed. "You look stunning," she stated.

A brief knock sounded at the suite door and then Vittorio and Constantine entered. Tears filled her father's eyes as he embraced her. And concern ripped the stoic mask from her brother's face. "Are you sure you want to go through with this?" he whispered as they embraced.

"I'm positive."

"It's time to go," Vittorio warned.

Ariana barely recalled the ride from Le Premier to the small, intimate church. The stone structure topped a hill close to downtown and offered a tantalizing glimpse of the bay with its dotting of islands and famous red bridge. Her mother and grandmother hugged and kissed her before proceeding into the chapel, leaving Ariana in the garden with her father.

The constant clamor of busy streets and bustling people faded away. In its place, a lush summer wind stirred her veil and voluminous skirts and caused the surrounding trees to creak and rustle. Birdsong rose and fell, sweet and life-affirming. And then came the joyful pealing of bells.

Vittorio tipped her chin up so their eyes met and held. "There's something you need to know before you marry Lazz."

"What is it, Papa? What's wrong?"

He hesitated, conflict rife on his face. "It's about Brimstone. It's—it's gone missing."

It took a second for his words to sink in. Once they had, she fought to breathe. Oh, please let her have misunderstood. "What do you mean…missing? How does a diamond go missing?"

"I can't find it anywhere," he confessed.

"You mean, you've lost it?" At his reluctant nod, she shook her head in distress. "I don't understand. Didn't you have it in a safe deposit box? Isn't it locked up?"

"It was." He glanced over to where the wedding co-ordinator beckoned to them, indicating it was time to enter the chapel. "There's no time to go into the details right now. Just believe me when I say that I'm doing everything I can to recover the stone."

"I still don't understand. Why are we going through with the wedding, Papa? Why didn't you stop it as soon as you realized Brimstone was missing? Why haven't you told the Dantes?"

He rushed into speech. "I just need time. Time to find it."

"We don't have any time," she reminded him. "My birthday is in two days. If Lazz and I aren't married by then, Brimstone will be disposed of—assuming, of course, you can find the diamond in order to dispose of it."

He nodded unhappily. "If you want to cancel the wedding, we will."

It was the only sensible option, Ariana conceded. But it also meant a tremendous loss should her father recover the diamond in the meantime. She thought fast. "What will happen to the family if I back out? How do you think the Dantes will respond?"

"We'd have to explain everything to Primo and your mother and grandmother."

Ariana crossed herself with a moan.

"Don't worry, *bambolina*. We'll find a way to work it out." But she couldn't help noticing he didn't quite meet her gaze. "I'm sure the Dantes will be reasonable about everything."

Right. After all, look how reasonable Lazz had been so far with all of his premarital conditions. Somehow she didn't see him being any more reasonable about the loss of the diamond. Her hands twisted together. What if the Dantes decided to take legal action? It would destroy her family and start a media frenzy. She and her father wouldn't be the only ones affected, either. Constantine would never be able to start his own business. And as for Gran… She'd already been through one media nightmare. She couldn't handle another. Even worse, if the Romanos were put under such intense scrutiny, someone might uncover her grandmother's secret identity.

"I'm going through with it," she informed her father. "That'll give you time to find the diamond. But I beg you, Papa, make it fast."

There wasn't time for more conversation. The wedding coordinator scurried out, grabbed the two by the hands and literally dragged them toward the chapel. "Hurry, please. We're late."

Ariana and Vittorio paused in the vestibule. He bent and kissed her before helping settle a layer of the tulle veil over her face. Together they entered the still coolness of the chapel. The bells gentled, replaced by the sweet welcome of strings heralding her approach.

Ariana struggled against a wave of emotion. In that moment, she didn't care why she'd agreed to this marriage or whether it had been a reasonable decision. Right now, she longed for more. All the trappings were here—the sanctity of the church, the beauty of the music, the warmth and well wishes of her family and Lazz's. But it wasn't real. It lacked the most important ingredient of all.

Love.

A man who looked exactly like Marco stood to one side of the altar, wearing a tux. No, she realized an instant later. He wasn't quite identical to Marco. As she approached, she could detect minute differences. Lazz was every bit as handsome as his twin, but lacked the mischievous twinkle and ready smile. This man remained guarded and implacable, watching her with a deep, penetrating intelligence.

There was depth there and an innate power, as well as a delicious sensuality that tugged at her the closer she came. A hum of tension grew with each step. By the time she joined him at the altar, the hum had escalated to a sizzle of awareness unlike anything she'd ever felt before. She fought to conceal it, to keep from trembling in reaction.

As though experiencing something similar, Lazz stiffened and fixed her with a fierce gaze. His eyes were a similar shade of hazel-green to Marco's, except that the green in Lazz's eyes appeared more intense, the gold highlights slightly tarnished. Somehow his gaze went deeper and saw far more, reflecting the heart of someone who had been badly burned in the past and chose to keep his distance from the flames in the future.

Time seemed to catch its breath as he studied her through the veiling layer of tulle. It felt as though he spoke to her on some private wavelength. As though some part of him called to her, demanding a response. She almost took that final step separating them, intent on wrapping herself around him. Before she could cave to instinct, Lazz cupped her elbow and turned them to face the priest, his touch burning through the satin of her sleeve.

The ceremony passed in a haze, the familiar words settling over her like a comforting mantle. Finally the moment came when they were to speak their vows. The priest blessed their rings and presented hers to Lazz. She watched as he accepted the simple gold band, fascinated by the graceful sweep of his hand. She'd never noticed Marco's hands before, but she did Lazz's. They were long and powerful and unbearably elegant. At the priest's direction, Lazz took her hand in his.

And that's when it happened.

She'd felt the burn of his touch through the satin of her wedding gown. But it was nothing in comparison to the shock that struck her when skin touched skin. It hit with such force that if Lazz hadn't been holding on to her, she'd have fallen. His fingers tightened around hers, and she glanced up, somewhat relieved to see his look of stunned disbelief. It would seem she wasn't the only one to feel it.

"What the hell was that?" he muttered.

"Not quite the first words I'd hoped to hear my husband speak," she whispered back. "But an excellent question. What just happened?"

With a swift glance toward the priest, Lazz shook his head and the ceremony resumed. He repeated his vows in a strong, clear voice. And then it was her turn. Whatever had caused the jolt of electricity had subsided into a bone-deep warmth that seeped inward and lapped through her veins, melting her into irrational want.

She struggled to focus on the words of commitment, but they turned into a meaningless jumble that twisted her tongue and had her switching impatiently to Italian. Sympathetic laughter drifted from those seated in the pews. No doubt they thought wedding jitters were responsible. But this—whatever *this* was— had nothing to do with jitters and everything to do with the man holding her hand.

Minutes flew by and then came the words she'd awaited with equal parts dread and anticipation. The priest pronounced his final blessing then instructed Lazz to kiss his bride. He took his time, driving her to the brink of insanity with his deliberation.

Slowly, he reached for her, capturing her veil and flipping it backward away from her face. He gazed down at her, his expression one of avid curiosity. It confirmed what she'd suspected. He didn't remember her. The time they'd been in Marco's conference room together hadn't made the least impression, no doubt because he'd been focused on his brother and Caitlyn— the woman Marco had tricked into marriage, as well as the woman Lazz had hoped to marry.

Perhaps if circumstances had been different, she'd have found Lazz's stunned reaction to her appearance amusing. Clearly, she met with his approval. As though unable to resist, he lowered his head and kissed her. She sensed he meant to keep it light and impersonal. But the instant their lips touched, heat exploded. His arms closed around her, powerful and possessive, and he locked her against him.

She'd been wrong. Oh, so wrong. Marco might have been a good kisser, but her husband was incredible.

One minute Lazz controlled both his life and destiny, and the next he took a woman he'd never truly met before for his wife and stepped into the vortex of a tornado.

If his life depended on it, he couldn't have said what had happened in the course of the past ten minutes. From the instant he took Ariana's hand in his own, everything changed. His illusion of control was ripped away, shredded in the howling winds of the tornado that tore through him. Reason vanished, as well. One thought consumed him.

Claim this woman. Grab hold of her and never let go.

He needed to make her his in every way possible. To make her understand that they were connected. That they belonged together. He vaguely heard the priest instruct him to kiss Ariana, and he wanted to shout in exultation.

First came the touch that linked them. Then came the kiss. And later, when they were alone, he would complete the bond between them. He would make her his in every sense of the word.

She trembled in his arms, but it wasn't fear that caused it. He could sense a hint of nervousness when he kissed her. Of surprise. Then it changed. The rapid pounding of her heart matched his, the passion blooming within her a mate for his own. Whatever the connection between them, it went both ways, a circuit completed.

And then, as though from a great distance, Lazz heard Marco in his capacity of best man. "I believe that's now Dantes zero," he murmured, just loud enough for Lazz to hear. "The Inferno four for four. Looks like the family blessing wins again."

The instant the words penetrated, he released Ariana and yanked himself free of the flames. No. Not a chance in hell. It couldn't be The Inferno. And yet, what other explanation could there be for what he felt? For his complete and utter loss of control? He'd never set eyes on Ariana before, at least not since she was a child of five, and yet it was as though he knew her. Worse than that, he wanted her with a wanton desperation he'd never experienced toward another woman.

She stared up at him with an expression of dazed bewilderment. "What just happened?" she asked in Italian.

"Absolutely nothing." He refused to even consider any other possibility.

They turned to face the congregation, and he saw a hint of amusement sparkle in her gaze, the same amusement he'd heard in her voice during the phone conversations they'd shared. "If that's 'nothing,' I can't wait to give 'something' a try."

They weren't given the opportunity for further conversation. Church bells rang out, and the strings began a joyous recessional. Ariana slipped her hand through Lazz's arm, and together they made their way down the aisle. As they passed the front pew, he caught a glimpse of his grandparents. Nonna dabbed at tears while Primo regarded him with an expression of such relief that Lazz nearly flinched.

Secrets and lies. He despised them, even as he lived them. He'd spent the last several months trying to convince himself that his reasons were sound, that recovering Brimstone was worth the minor inconvenience of a temporary marriage. But looking at his grandfather, Lazz knew that Primo would never have approved his decision, not if it meant consigning a hundred Brimstones to the deep blue sea. There was only one way of winning Primo's approval.

Lazz would have to marry his Inferno mate.

As though picking up on his thoughts, Ariana leaned in. "What happened when we first touched?" she asked in an undertone.

"Like I said. Nothing." The denial came automatically. It was another lie or, more likely, a hope. He escorted her to the limousine waiting to drive them to their reception at Le Premier. The driver opened the door while Lazz helped his bride in.

The instant the door enclosed them in dusky privacy, she shifted to face him. "That wasn't nothing. When you took my hand, you shocked me," she argued. "And don't try and tell me it was static electricity."

"It was static electricity."

Instead of arguing, she smiled. "Have it your way. When you're ready to tell me the truth, let me know."

"There's nothing to tell."

She leaned closer, and he struggled to keep his hands off her, to keep himself from kissing her again. He longed to see if what they'd experienced before was a onetime deal or an insanity he could expect every time they touched. "In case you haven't noticed," she told him, "you've already broken your first marital condition. No secrets, remember?"

Son of a— "This isn't the appropriate time."

"Of course not," she instantly agreed. "Though your comment suggests there is…something."

"Delicately put. And yes, there is something. But it has nothing to do with us. Nothing to do with what happened at the church." He refused to even consider the possibility.

"And what did happen at the church?"

"We kissed." And time stopped. The gates to heaven opened. And the earth moved—without benefit of an earthquake.

To his relief, the limousine pulled up in front of the hotel, putting an end to their discussion. Their marriage was temporary, he reminded himself. He'd be a fool to expect anything else, to complicate a simple, straightforward agreement with whatever form of lunacy held him in its grip, especially considering Ariana's marital conditions.

Once inside, they joined the wedding party in a receiving line. No sooner were they free from that duty when the orchestra began the opening strands of a waltz. Lazz took Ariana's hand in his and led her out onto the floor for the opening dance. Applause drifted through the assembled guests as the bridal couple circled the room. But Lazz might as well have been deaf and blind to everyone but the woman he held close to his heart.

She fit in his arms as though the universe had deliberately formed her as his perfect counterpart. A deep melding formed where their palms joined, a melding he'd often heard his brothers refer to. Even so, he refused to believe it was The Inferno.

He'd felt a similar tingling before in Caitlyn's presence the day after she'd married Marco. Granted, it hadn't been this strong. Not even close. But he refused to give in to the family delusion, to pretend that whatever he felt toward his temporary wife could be anything more than simple, ordinary lust. He'd accepted long ago that fairy tales weren't meant for him. And who wouldn't have reacted to Ariana? His wife was a beautiful woman.

Lazz gazed down at her. Incredibly beautiful, he corrected. Stunning. Her face contained an intriguing mixture of lushness and delicacy. And while her features were fine-boned and aristocratic, her mouth was full and ripe and the exact color of sun-kissed peaches. She gazed up at him with sweetly wanton eyes that exactly matched the deep, rich brown of bittersweet chocolate. Even her skin revealed the complexity of her nature, passion giving a rosy glow to the creamy white blending of her Latin heritage with her British.

"Have I told you how beautiful you look?" The words escaped of their own volition.

"Thank you. I can't take credit for it. It was an accident of birth."

He laughed. "That was one hell of an accident."

"You appeared surprised when you lifted the veil. Why?"

"I'd never seen you before. Well, not since we were children," he corrected.

An odd expression drifted across her face, part pain and part exasperation. "That's not true. We were in the same room together not so many months ago."

Lazz stared. "Are you serious?"

"Quite serious."

"Not a chance," he denied. "If we'd met that recently, I'd have remembered. When was this? Where?"

Ariana stared at a spot over his shoulder. She'd known at the time that he hadn't noticed her, even as she'd felt the first shimmer of a connection. It hadn't been anywhere near as strong as at the church. But it had definitely been there.

She shouldn't take it personally that he didn't remember her. She'd seen how he'd reacted to the news of Caitlyn's marriage to Marco. It had devastated Lazz, a fact he'd driven home by physically attacking his brother. She wouldn't have been a female worthy of the name if she hadn't understood that both twins had been in love with the same woman.

"Ariana?"

"It was at Dantes. In Marco's conference room." She forced herself to look at him, allowing her gaze to reflect the full depth of her knowledge. "The morning after Caitlyn's marriage to Marco."

It was as though an impenetrable barrier slammed into place. "You were there?"

She couldn't help but laugh, though the sound carried a hint of sorrow. "I believe that explains why you don't remember me. Did you love her very much? Are you still in love with her?"

"She's my sister-in-law."

"That doesn't answer my questions."

"As my wife—as my temporary wife—that subject doesn't concern us. It has nothing to do with our marriage, the contract that brought us together or the conditions we both agreed to before marrying."

So cool. So logical. And yet, she sensed that emotion smoldered just beneath the surface, like dry tinder longing for a hot spark to set it ablaze. "What about our agreement not to keep secrets?"

"Consider the subject of Caitlyn to be the equivalent of your privacy room."

"Ah."

"What does that mean?"

She shrugged. "It just means that I understand." Then she added a gentle, "And sympathize."

"I didn't ask—" He broke off, staring toward a cluster of his relatives. "What's going on over there?"

Ariana turned to look. "That's Nicolò and…Kiley? Do I have her name right?"

"Yes. Aw, hell. They're all crying. We need to get over there. Something's wrong."

A chuckle escaped Ariana. "Nothing's wrong. Not unless having a baby is wrong."

"A baby!"

"See how Nonna is touching Kiley's belly? That's

universal woman-speak. And now Francesca is…" Her laughter grew. "Oh, how sweet. Please, can we go over and congratulate both of them?"

"Both. Both?"

"Francesca and Kiley. I wonder how close their due dates are."

She caught Lazz's hand in hers and urged him toward where the Dantes stood gathered. With everyone talking and laughing at once, it took a moment for them to be absorbed into the group. The minute Ariana reached her sisters-in-law, she gave each a hug in turn.

"I didn't mean to steal your thunder," Kiley instantly said. "But Nonna took one look at me and burst into tears. And as soon as Francesca understood why, she started to cry. And well…"

"Why would you apologize? You have made our special day all the more joyous. May I?" At Kiley's nod, Ariana spread her hand over Kiley's abdomen. "For good luck and God's blessing. Have you been trying long?"

"We weren't trying at all." A blush touched Kiley's cheeks. "I was nearly run down by an SUV when I ran into the street to save Nicolò's dog. Afterward, he and I… Well, one thing led to another and somewhere on our journey between the one thing and the other, we forgot a few vital steps, steps that ended up with me pregnant. Not that I'm complaining."

"You're happy then?"

Kiley reached for Nicolò's hand and tears filled her eyes. "Ecstatic."

Ariana turned to give Francesca another hug of congratulations. "I don't have to ask how you feel. You're glowing."

Francesca chuckled. "I couldn't be happier. Maybe that's because I'm not suffering from morning sickness the way Kiley is."

"It will end soon," Nonna offered.

Primo caught his wife's hand in his. "And do you see boys or girls in their future?"

"Boys for these two." Her gaze landed on Ariana, her eyes eerily similar to Lazz's. Then her face lit up. "But you. You will have a daughter. The only Dante girl of your generation, I'm sad to say."

"Nonna—" Lazz began.

Ariana shushed him before giving Nonna a swift hug. "You have the sight? My great-grandmother Romano did, as well. Everything she predicted always came true. This is her veil I'm wearing."

"Nonna predicted my pregnancy," Francesca warned. "So, I'd start knitting little pink booties, if I were you."

"I'll get right on it. But after the honeymoon if you don't mind," Ariana teased. To her surprise, even Lazz laughed.

"I am glad you mentioned the honeymoon," Primo said. "Penelope, Nonna and I all have a small surprise for the two of you. Lazz, I know you said there is no time for a honeymoon right now, but I have made arrangements for Caitlyn to fill in for you while you and Ariana go away."

Beside her, Lazz stiffened. "You shouldn't have—" he began, before being waved silent by his grandfather.

"These past six months have been long and difficult for you." Fierce golden eyes gazed at his grandson with compassion. "You deserve a break."

"The Romanos are well acquainted with the royal families of Verdonia," Penelope contributed. "So, we've arranged for you to stay there. Your flight leaves tomorrow."

"What a lovely gesture," Ariana said. "Thank you so much. You're all too generous."

Lazz added his thanks to her own, then kissed his grandparents, as well as Penelope. Only Vittorio didn't contribute to the celebration. Ariana sensed his concern and did her best to alleviate it with a cheerful demeanor. So long as he found Brimstone before Lazz uncovered their deception, all would be fine. Otherwise… She shuddered. She didn't want to consider the alternatives.

The minute she and Lazz were alone again, she regarded him with a hint of uncertainty. "You don't seem as upset as I expected you to be."

"I'm not."

"You surprise me."

He lifted a shoulder in a casual shrug. "This gives us time to get to know each other. By the time we return, we'll be more relaxed together."

"Like an old married couple?"

"Something like that." He lifted an eyebrow. "Now you're the one who looks upset. You knew we were going to have to convince our grandparents that we're happily married before gradually going our separate ways. This will help the process along."

"They're going to find out eventually," she murmured.

"They'll find out that the marriage didn't work out. They won't find out why we married in the first place."

"They'd be crushed if they knew."

"Knowing Primo, he'd dispose of Brimstone just to make that point." Lazz inclined his head toward the head table. "Recess is over, I'm afraid. Time to resume our duties."

The rest of the reception passed with a breathtaking swiftness. Before she knew it, Lazz caught her hand and drew her from the ballroom onto a shadow-dipped balcony overlooking downtown San Francisco. When she shot him a questioning glance, he merely smiled.

"They expect us to leave early. We're supposed to be eager newlyweds, remember?"

She shook her head in amusement. "How silly of me. Of course. We'd probably shock our guests if we insisted on dancing the night away. Still…" She crossed to the railing and gazed out at the glittering lights of the city. Fog stretched out stealthy fingers, reaching for the streets closest to the bay. "It was a lovely reception. Thank you for putting it together."

"I didn't—"

"Please, don't." Her smile faltered for an instant before she had it safely back in place. "Please, don't tell me you weren't responsible. I'd like that much of an illusion, if you don't mind."

"Actually, I was going to say that I didn't expect it to turn out as well as it did," he said gently. "And I was responsible, though I had help."

"From Caitlyn?"

"Among others. Come on." He dropped an arm around her shoulders. "Le Premier has reserved the honeymoon suite for us tonight."

"And tomorrow we fly off to Verdonia," she said, hoping her nervousness didn't show. "I guess that means we better get a decent night's sleep. Tomorrow's flight will be a long one."

"Then I suggest we turn in." His face slid into shadow, while ambient light caught in the depths of his hazel eyes. "And when we get to our room, you can decide whether you'd care to break one of your marital conditions."

Three

From: Bambolina@fornitore.it
Date: 2008, August 05 18:41 CEST
To: Lazzaro_Dante@DantesJewelry.com
Subject: Re: Marriage Contract, Premarital Conditions...**mine!**

Dear Lazzaro,

I'm sure you will understand the need for my first counter-condition, especially since our marriage is not permanent.

Counter-Condition #1: No sex.

Short and sweet, yes?

Ciao! Ariana

P.S. I guess that means we'll need separate bedrooms. Do you wish me to make that a separate counter-condition?

Ariana didn't say a word. Not as they left the balcony, nor during the endless elevator ride to their suite. She didn't dare speak in the face of such overwhelming temptation.

She hadn't expected such a strong physical response to Lazz. Perhaps she should have, since she'd been drawn to him every single time she'd been in his presence, starting at the tender age of five. When she'd seen him in Marco's conference room, some part of her had instinctively sensed the connection between them. She'd even told her father that Lazz was the one.

The one she'd cried over at five.

The one who called to her on some visceral level.

The one who'd connected them with a single touch.

"Looks like someone's been here ahead of us," Lazz commented as they entered the suite.

Sure enough, flowers covered every available surface, including the huge canopied bed, although in the case of the bed they were deep velvety red petals, with a pair of long-stem roses decorating the pillows.

"I don't see luggage anywhere," she said. "Should we ring for it?"

A hint of a smile carved a path across Lazz's mouth. "I'm guessing no one thought you would need luggage until tomorrow. Other than this…" He snagged a swath of virtually transparent ivory silk that had been spread across the down duvet topping their bed. He lifted an eyebrow. "Do you need help changing?"

Oh, heaven help her. Surely, she hadn't been left with just her wedding gown and…and that. Ariana cleared her throat. "I think I mentioned that my mother doesn't know that we're not—" She gave an expressive shrug. "I'm sure she meant it as a romantic gesture."

Tossing her nightgown to the bed, he proceeded to strip off his tux jacket. "I don't have any objections. Nor am I offended." He ripped his tie free of its mooring, allowing the ribbon of black silk to flutter to the carpet. "And you still haven't answered my question. Either of my questions, for that matter."

If he'd asked any questions, she'd already forgotten. His unnerving striptease had driven them straight out of her head. "I'm sorry…?"

A hungry smile slipped across his face. He worked the onyx studs free of his shirt and dropped them onto the bedside table. "Do you need help undressing?" he prompted. "And how soon can we break your first marital condition?"

It took a heartbeat to force her gaze from his gaping shirt and the broad expanse of golden chest beneath. Another heartbeat to gather her wits enough to respond. "Yes, as a matter of fact, I do need help undressing."

She crossed to Lazz's side with as much composure as she could summon. There was something about a half-undressed man that struck her as downright dangerous to the female psyche, particularly when the other half was clothed in formal wear. Maybe it was the incongruity she found so appealing. Somehow she'd have to find a way to ignore it, though she didn't have a clue how. Not when a relentless tug of desire attacked all her senses at once, leaving her totally defenseless.

Presenting her back to him, she asked, "Would you mind unbuttoning my gown?"

"My pleasure. And you still haven't answered my other question."

He stroked a hand down the length of her spine. Even through the heavy satin of the material, she could feel the heat of his touch. Feel the tautening of the connection between them. "The answer is never," she managed to say. "I don't intend to break any of my premarital conditions."

"Or allow me to?"

"No." Yes, please. Soon and often.

"Are you certain?"

She fought to control her shudder of awareness. More than anything, she wanted to throw herself in his arms and beg him to make love to her. To complete whatever odd bond had formed between them during their wedding ceremony. But she couldn't. She wouldn't.

"I'm positive."

To her relief, he accepted her response without argument though she could sense that he forcibly held himself in check. "I have to admit, this is a first for me," he admitted. "I've never helped a woman out of a wedding gown before."

"I wish you hadn't told me that."

"Why?"

She felt the subtle give of her gown. "It makes me sad."

"Sad, that you're the first I've ever stripped out of a wedding gown?" A hint of amusement ran through his words. The back of his hand brushed against her skin, eliciting a shiver she couldn't quite suppress. "I would think that would make you happy."

"I'm not your true bride, or it would. It makes me sad thinking of your future wife and the fact that all the things that should be a first with her are a first with me, instead." She twisted around, holding her gown against her breasts. In the short time her back had been to him, a darkness had wiped all emotion from his face, turning it remote and forbidding. "Perhaps I'm not phrasing it well," she murmured.

"You phrased it just fine."

"I've annoyed you. I am sorry."

"Not at all." He made a circle with his finger, a silent demand that she turn around again. "I'm not quite done."

"Oh, of course." She did as he requested, forcing herself to stand perfectly still while he finished unbuttoning her gown. "It's just that these little memories should be special. I don't want to tarnish them."

He'd reached the last button, but instead of releasing her, he cupped her hips and slid her tight against him. Her breath escaped in a silent gasp, and she froze as his bare chest pressed against her bare back, heat against heat. One hand slid from her hip to settle low on her abdomen where one day she hoped a child would nestle. Desire intensified, driving her nearly insane with need. She could feel the strong, tensed muscles of his thighs and knew he was aroused. Seriously aroused. Knew that she'd done that to him, just as he'd done the same to her.

"What about you?" he asked. An almost guttural quality slid through his voice. "Am I tarnishing sacred memories for you and your future husband?"

"No, because this isn't real." But it felt real. His

hands on her. Their partial nudity. The want that thickened the air and made it difficult to breathe. A wedding night waiting to happen. It felt all too real. "Someday I'll have a real marriage. But this isn't it. It can't be."

"It can, if you let it." He spun her around. "Let's start with that kiss we shared. Let's find out whether that was real…or pure imagination."

And then he took her mouth in a kiss reserved for lovers, one that claimed, just as it seduced. A kiss that proved that what they'd felt earlier hadn't been imagination, not unless they were both experiencing the exact same fantasy. Time seemed to halt, to give them endless seconds to wallow in the moment. This man could have brought stone to life, Ariana decided, and she was far from stone. If she could have melded her body to his, she would have. Instead, she simply gave everything she had within her. And then she gave more.

He slid his fingers deep into her hair as he consumed her, tumbling them from one delicious connection into the next. "I don't give a damn what we agreed. I need you."

And she needed him. Needed the hardness of his mouth over hers. Needed the delicious blaze of heat. She wanted to fill her lungs with his breath, to inhale his scent and taste and revel in the very air that sustained him.

Every nerve in her body screamed in surrender, making it almost impossible to resist the inevitable. Somehow she managed. "We have an agreement." The words were barely more than a whisper.

He pulled back just far enough to allow sanity to slip between them. "An agreement…or a suggestion?"

"It was an agreement you promised to honor," she insisted. "Please let go of me."

He bent his head and buried a final kiss in the sensitive curve between her neck and shoulder. Fire flashed through her, arrowing from her breasts straight to the warm feminine core of her, and a deep yearning threatened all she held most dear. "No one needs to know." The words hovered, tantalizing with possibility.

"I would know." Could he feel how she trembled? Could he sense her longing? She needed to stop him while she could still stop herself. She spoke with difficulty, fighting to translate her thoughts into English. And still her tongue stumbled over the words. "And it would prevent us from getting an annulment. Since we were married in the church, and since Romanos don't believe in divorce, we can't take this any further."

To her profound relief—or was it regret?—he released her. "If that's your preference."

She clutched the bodice of her gown to her breasts to keep it from slipping. "It is." Not. Most decidedly, not. She didn't dare look at him in case her conflicted emotions showed on her face. "I'll use the bathroom first, if you don't mind."

"Fine." He stopped her with a touch, one that raced across her skin like wildfire. "Fair warning, Mrs. Dante. There's only one bed, and I'm not feeling terribly chivalrous, particularly with the flight we have to look forward to tomorrow. I hope you don't mind sharing."

"Not at all." She spared the bed a brief, wistful glance. "It's large enough to house an entire family. We'll just stake out opposite sides."

By the time she removed her wedding gown and used the toiletries supplied by the hotel, she managed to gather up the tattered remains of her equilibrium. She also managed to silence her wayward body and the wicked suggestions it screamed by drowning every hungry inch in an icy shower. Though she attempted to convince herself otherwise, the remnants of his touch remained, soft echoes of helpless passion.

She smothered the echoes beneath a luxurious Le Premier bathrobe, one that enveloped her sheer nightgown. She emerged from the bathroom to find Lazz relaxing in the bed, reading a newspaper. The fact that he was quite likely nude beneath the sheets—after all, her mother hadn't left any nighttime garments for him—threw her enough that she spoke in Italian instead of English.

"Ah, the perfect picture of domestic bliss," she teased.

He glanced up and returned her grin, though she suspected it had more to do with the voluminous bathrobe than her comment. "I put a buffer between us," he said, indicating the line of pillows that divided the bed. "I hope it will make you feel more comfortable."

"I assume you're a man of your word?"

"Of course."

She grabbed the pillows and tossed them to the floor. "Then I trust you without these."

As soon as she'd stripped off the bathrobe and climbed into bed, he turned out the light. At first the darkness seemed impenetrable. But gradually her eyesight adjusted, and she managed to make out the various pieces of furniture scattered around the suite. She also managed to make out her husband's form. Other than tossing aside the newspaper, he hadn't altered his position. He continued to lounge against a mountain of pillows, his arms folded behind his head. In the darkness his breathing seemed deep and heavy. Hungry. Teetering on the edge of action.

She rushed into speech before opportunity became deed. "You know, you never explained what happened in the church. What caused that shock when we touched?"

"As I said before, it wasn't anything."

She sat up in order to plump her pillows and adjust the bedding. Nerves. Nerves were making her restless and chatty. Maybe she should have had that second glass of champagne she'd been offered during the endless round of toasts. It might have helped her sleep. She spared Lazz a swift glance. Or maybe not. No telling what foolish decisions she'd be tempted to make while under the influence.

"And yet, you also said there was something you weren't telling me," she persisted. "When we were in the limousine, remember?"

"It's nothing. A family legend."

"A legend? That sounds interesting." She wriggled around in an effort to find a comfortable spot in the massive bed. Since the most comfortable spot was in Lazz's arms, she didn't expect to meet with much success. Exasperated, she said, "Since I'm not sleeping and you're not sleeping, why don't you tell me about it."

"I'm surprised you haven't already heard. But perhaps you don't read gossip magazines."

"I have read a few," she admitted. "*The Snitch.* But

when Papa came across it, he was furious and banned the paper from the estate. Since then I've been gossip free."

"Well, that explains it." Lazz fell silent, and for a brief moment Ariana wondered if he'd decided against telling her his "secret." Not that she didn't sympathize, considering she had a few of her own. And then he spoke. "Our family claims an odd sort of legacy. I consider it a not-so-charming fairy tale."

"But some of your family think this legacy is real?"

"Yes. It's called The Inferno."

She instantly clicked on the play on words. "Dantes' Inferno? I love it. What is this Inferno? And who in your family believes in it?"

"Most of them," he admitted. Reluctance tore through his words. "I don't know about my cousins, but all of my brothers claim to have experienced it. In fact, Primo and Nonna are under the impression we're marrying because of The Inferno, and I intend to keep it that way."

"I gather you don't believe in it?"

"Not even a little."

"Yet, you expect us to pretend we feel it?"

"Yes."

Ariana rubbed her thumb against the center of her palm where the spark between them had first originated and where the heat from it still seemed to dwell. That spark hadn't been nothing, despite what Lazz might claim. Could it be from this Inferno Lazz insisted didn't exist? It would certainly explain a lot.

"How can I pretend to feel The Inferno if I don't know what it is?" she asked with a touch of his logic. "Won't your grandparents expect me to know?"

"Yeah. I didn't think of that, but they will expect it." He shifted in the bed, rolling over to face her. Darkness hid his expression from her, but not his scent. Not his size. Not the fascinating ridges and valleys his body created beneath the sheets. Those were all too apparent. "It's…it's a connection. A bond. My brothers claim they experienced it the first time they touched their wives."

Ariana's breath caught in sudden understanding. "And if I asked them, would they say The Inferno felt something like an electric shock?"

"They might," Lazz conceded. "According to my brothers, after they touched, they were so overcome with desire, they couldn't think straight."

"Unlike what we felt in church. You were completely in control when you kissed me, right?"

She could practically hear him grind his teeth at her irony. "You're a beautiful woman. It's only natural that I'd be sexually attracted to you. It has nothing to do with The Inferno. The Inferno isn't real."

"Is it that The Inferno isn't real? Or is it that you consider yourself too logical to experience it?"

"It isn't real. I am logical. Therefore, how could I possibly experience it? What my brothers felt toward their wives is simple lust, nothing more. They chose to call it The Inferno because it puts a polite word to emotions that are more carnal than romantic."

She pounced on the flaw in his argument. "Then explain what happened when we first touched. Or didn't you feel what I did?"

"I felt something. But it wasn't because of some ridiculous legend."

A sudden idea occurred to Ariana, and she fought

to speak without inflection. "Do you deny it because you experienced this Inferno with Caitlyn? Do you believe you can't feel that with another woman?"

"It's only supposed to happen with one woman. I thought I felt something with her," Lazz confessed. "Once. It happened—" He broke off, swearing beneath his breath.

"What?" She sat up in bed. "I don't understand. When did it happen?"

"It doesn't matter."

"It does matter," she insisted. "When did it happen?"

"The morning after she married Marco."

"In the conference room? When you attacked your brother?" When she and her father had been there to witness the fight? When she'd been seized by that overpowering attraction to Lazz?

"Yes. But what happened that day doesn't have anything to do with us or our situation. Or, God forbid, The Inferno."

His words shouldn't hurt. For some reason, they did. "Because ours is a temporary marriage, right?" She didn't wait for a response. "Just out of curiosity, what are you looking for in a wife, if not The Inferno?"

Lazz hesitated long enough that Ariana thought he wouldn't answer. And then he said, "I'd rather have a marriage based on compatibility. On reason. On mutual likes and dislikes. Once emotion subsides, there has to be something to keep the marriage together. All The Inferno offers is physical desire. I want more than that."

Is that what he'd found with Caitlyn? "And yet, it seems to have worked out for your brothers. I gather you believe you have some sort of special immunity, is that it?"

Lazz moved with lightning speed. One minute he lounged safely next to her and the next Ariana found herself caged beneath him. He interlaced their fingers, and she felt again that odd burn within her palm. Not that he seemed to notice. But then, maybe he was distracted by the way he anchored her body to the mattress, filling her soft contours with hard male angles, forcing her to give to his take. His take of space. His take of control. He even seemed to take the air she fought to pull into her lungs.

"Listen to me, Ariana. What you and I felt earlier was a natural desire. If you want to pursue that desire to its natural conclusion, I'd be delighted to accommodate you." He freed a hand and used it to cup her breast. His thumb drifted across the hardened peak, showing her without words how easily and how well that accommodation would be. "But don't expect anything more than the conditions we both agreed to."

His words doused the desire screaming through her body. "Thank you for making that clear." She made the mistake of speaking in Italian again and deliberately switched to English. "If you don't mind, I think I'll go to sleep now."

His tantalizing movements stilled. "I assume you prefer to do that without me on top of you?"

"You assume correctly."

He lowered his head and skated his mouth across hers. Just a light, tender brush of lips against lips. Her groan slipped out as he slipped in. He told her without words how it could be between them, showed her with a simple mating of their mouths and tongues how he would turn her world upside down.

But where would that leave her afterward? She'd have given everything and been left with nothing but heartache. Lazz didn't believe in the possibilities or in the connection that had sparked to life between them. And a night in his arms, no matter how blissful, wouldn't change that.

"I gather the answer is still no."

Ariana didn't trust herself to speak, not with the frantic words fighting for release. Words that would beg him to hold her. To make love to her. To give her a wedding night she'd never forget. But it would only add complications on top of complications, especially with Brimstone missing. She pushed against his shoulders, still unable to reply. He rolled off of her without another word.

She didn't expect to sleep, not considering her intense awareness of the man beside her and not with her emotions in such turmoil. Not only did she long to give in to base instinct but she also knew that part of her, a secret childish part, wished that she could experience The Inferno with Lazz.

She couldn't help but wonder if maybe, just maybe, the reaction she had to his touch—and his response to hers—might mean that her secret wish had come true. What if the odd sensations they'd shared were from The Inferno? How would that change her plans for the future?

And how did she convince her husband that his plans for the future should change, too?

The instant Lazz and Ariana's plane touched down in Verdonia, they were whisked by limousine through the mountainous principality of Avernos to the private estate of the newly elected king, Brandt von Folke.

"According to my grandmother, King Brandt was elected about eighteen months ago," Ariana said.

Lazz lifted an eyebrow . "Elected? I gather succession doesn't follow hereditary lines in Verdonia."

"No, it doesn't. Here, they gather up all the eligible royals and have an election by the people. King Brandt won. My grandparents knew his grandfather, King Grandon. We used to visit when I was a child."

"Which explains your family's ability to pull a few royal strings and arrange our honeymoon trip."

"Exactly."

The car pulled up to the front of an enormous structure, part palace and part fortress. Hewn from local stone, it offered a hard, cold welcome in complete opposition to their reception by Brandt and Miri von Folke, both of whom Ariana remembered having met as a child.

After the formal introductions, Brandt arranged for refreshments and then surprised them by waving aside their use of his title. "There's no need," he insisted. "This isn't a state function, and I have as little interest in titles as my grandfather."

A baby of close to a year crawled over to Ariana and held out his arms imperiously. The minute she acquiesced and gathered him up, he gazed around and beamed in delight. "And who is this little one?" she asked in amusement.

"Thomas Grandon," Miri replied. "He's named after Brandt's father and grandfather. My brother, Lander, and his wife, Juliana, have a little girl the same age.

And we're expecting a call any minute from my brother, Merrick, about his wife, Alyssa. When he phoned a few hours ago, she was in labor."

As though in response to her comment, the door opened and a huge man appeared in the doorway. "A call for you, Your Highness. It's Prince Merrick."

"Thanks, Tolken." Miri shot to her feet. "This is it. I'll be right back. Oh, I hope Alyssa and the baby are safe and healthy."

Brandt reassured her with a simple touch. "They're fine. Now go and find out whether we have a new niece or nephew." He smiled at Ariana and Lazz. "They decided to be old-fashioned and keep the sex a surprise. Miri's been on pins and needles for months."

"I hope our arrival hasn't inconvenienced you," Lazz said. "We appreciate your allowing us to use your private cabin for our honeymoon."

Brandt waved that aside. "It's the perfect spot. The original cabin burned down a while back. We've replaced it, though this one is a bit snug."

Ariana shot a nervous glance in Lazz's direction. Just how snug was snug? "I'm sure it'll be perfect."

"I have fond memories of the place. Miri and I…" He broke off with a smile that turned his face from austere to warm and approachable. "Well, let's just say that our stay there changed our lives."

"Thank you so much for sharing it with us," Ariana murmured.

"Our pleasure." He rubbed his hands together. "Now, let me just go over a few particulars. The cabin is fully stocked for the week you'll be there. We've had electricity installed, but it goes down at the least provocation. There's a generator and propane to fuel it." He lifted an eyebrow in Lazz's direction. "Are you familiar with running a generator?"

"My family has a cabin that requires a generator. We were all taught how to work it—as well as maintain it—from an early age."

"Perfect. The generator is powerful enough to keep the refrigerator and freezer going, should you lose power. Tolken will arrange to provide you with cell phones. Again, the mountains make reception spotty, and this time of year our mountains send us some rather spectacular storms. I should warn you that they hit fast and hard. But I'll have someone call in a warning so they don't catch you off guard."

Lazz inclined his head. "Much appreciated."

"As soon as you're refreshed, I've arranged for my helicopter to fly you out and drop you off."

Ariana stiffened, fighting to conceal her alarm. "The cabin isn't accessible by car?"

"By four-wheel and even then with difficulty." He lifted a single eyebrow, and Ariana was painfully aware of his royal status. "Is that a problem?"

"Not at all," Lazz interrupted smoothly. "I can't think of a better way to spend our honeymoon."

Ariana forced an enthusiastic smile. "Nor can I."

Miri appeared just then, saving them from an awkward moment. "A boy. Eight pounds, two ounces," she announced in a breathless rush. Tears gathered in her eyes. "They've named him Stefan, after our father."

"He was our former king," Brandt explained in a low tone. "And succeeded my grandfather. His death was a great loss to all of us."

"I'm sure he would have been so proud to have his legacy continue," Ariana offered gently.

Brandt gave her a look of quiet approval before turning to his wife and gathering her close. "Would you care to freshen up before your departure?" he asked them.

It was clearly a dismissal, though one Ariana completely understood. This was an intimate moment. A time for family. For some reason, it caused her to slip her hand into Lazz's. She could feel the tug of the peculiar bond that had formed between them. He might deny that it was The Inferno, but whatever the link, it hummed with urgency.

"We can freshen up at the cabin," Lazz said. "We'll go ahead and leave you now."

The comment made Ariana smile, since she'd been about to say the same thing. "Please extend our good wishes to Prince Merrick and Princess Alyssa. It was a pleasure to see you both again after all these years." She crouched beside Thomas and ruffled his dark hair. "And it was especially nice to meet you, Prince Thomas."

Tolken returned a few minutes later and escorted them to the waiting chopper. "Your luggage is already loaded." He handed them a leather satchel. "This contains a pair of cell phones with emergency contact numbers. Don't hesitate to call if you need anything. King Brandt has put me entirely at your disposal."

Lazz offered his hand. "Thank you. If you don't hear from us, we'll see you in a week."

Tolken shook hands and then assisted Ariana into her seat and helped her strap in. A few minutes later, the helicopter lifted off the ground. It hovered over the estate for a few minutes, affording them a gorgeous bird's-eye view of the palace and grounds before banking northward.

The surrounding mountains were a deep, lush green with towering conifers and a scattering of oak, beech and alder. Eventually, they soared over one of the higher mountain peaks and drifted down toward a large clearing beside a sparkling green lake. White imported sand cupped the side closest to a small cabin. A very small cabin, Ariana noticed.

After touchdown, the pilot gave them a hand with their luggage. "Is there anything else I can do for you before heading back?" he asked.

"I think we can manage from here," Lazz assured him.

"The generator is housed in the shed over there." The pilot pointed toward a structure that abutted the edge of the forest. "And you'll find fishing gear in the boathouse down by the lake."

"Sounds fantastic."

The pilot lifted two fingers to his brow in a casual salute. "Enjoy yourself. If you need anything, I'm only a phone call away."

Lazz opened the door to the cabin and carried the luggage inside, but Ariana waited, watching as their only connection to civilization slowly rose. Its blades flattened the grass and kicked up small dirt devils before it tilted to one side and zipped southward on its return flight. A moment later, the earsplitting thump of the blade faded away as the helicopter vanished over the nearest mountaintop.

Ariana released her breath in a sigh and turned to

enter the cabin. It took her eyes a moment to adjust from the bright sunlight to the shadowed duskiness of the interior. The minute her vision cleared, she shook her head in disbelief.

"Call him back," she demanded in Italian. "There's no way I'm staying here."

Four

From: Lazzaro_Dante@DantesJewelry.com
Date: 2008, August 05 09:54 PDST
To: Bambolina@fornitore.it
Subject: Marriage Contract, Premarital Conditions, Additional

I think you're kidding yourself if you think either of us can go without sex for three whole months. I suggest you reconsider. And no, you don't need to make separate bedrooms a separate counter-condition. That's a given. In the meantime, here's my next premarital condition.

Condition #3: Occasional displays of public affection may be necessary in order to maintain the facade of a "normal" marriage.

L.

From: Bambolina@fornitore.it
Date: 2008, August 05 19:06 CEST
To: Lazzaro_Dante@DantesJewelry.com
Subject: Re: Marriage Contract, Premarital Conditions, Additional

Allow me to assure you that I am not kidding myself. I take sex very seriously. My first condition stands. *Capito?*

As for condition #3... Just what sort of public displays do you have in mind? I have the distinct impression your idea of a "normal" marriage and mine are quite different.

Ciao! Ariana

Lazz folded his arms across his chest. "We are not calling him back."

"I can't stay here with you." She waved her hand to indicate the interior of the cabin. "It's too... Too..."

"Intimate?"

"Yes!" She glanced at the bed and swiftly away again. "That mattress is barely big enough for one, let alone two. I thought kings had giant beds. *King-size* beds."

Lazz lifted an eyebrow at her phrasing, and a broad smile came and went. "Never having been a king, I can't say. I assume, considering how isolated this place is, they elected to stick with sizes that were easily transported. Or maybe Brandt and Miri prefer sleeping on top of each other."

She spared the bed a final, uneasy look. "Lazz—" she began.

He shook his head, adamant. "Forget it, Ariana. We're not going to refuse von Folke's hospitality. It would be rude, and word of it would get back to our grandparents."

That stopped her. She stared at him, stricken. "But what are we going to do?"

"We're going to do just what we agreed before our marriage. We're going to make the best of it."

"I can't even turn around without bumping into you."

"Bump into me as much as you like. I can live with it."

In fact, the idea appealed. A lot. The tension between them had already climbed to unbearable levels. At some point one of them would trip over that condition of hers and they'd both take a fall—preferably onto the nearest bed, no matter how narrow. As far as he was concerned, the sooner, the better.

She hesitated, no doubt wanting to react to the comment. He sensed his darling wife—and how he stumbled over *that* word—felt as edgy as he did. Their wedding night had been rough, the awareness they'd felt toward each other both unexpected and surprising, and not an issue either of them had anticipated dealing with. Although, if he were honest, he should have anticipated it. When two people were locked in a marriage, it was only natural that a severe case of intimacy was bound to break out at some point or another.

Now they'd gotten themselves into a situation they couldn't escape…a situation that threatened to break more than one of the conditions the two of them had made before their marriage. He could only hope his lasted longer than hers. Lazz studied Ariana and realized with a kick of amusement that she continued to hover by the door.

"You look like you're on the verge of running," he said.

"I'm considering it."

"Why don't you come on in and take a look around?"

Her expression soured. "I think I can pretty much see everything from here."

"It's supposed to be a romantic getaway, which may explain why there's more bedroom than anything else." He inclined his head toward the shadowed interior. "There's a small kitchen and a huge bathroom with a tiled shower stall and a tub that's larger than the bed."

"Maybe I can sleep in there." She turned her attention to the stone fireplace and the small sitting area that contained a deep love seat and a striking table made of a variety of inlaid hardwoods. "Very cozy."

"It's only for a week."

"I'm being ungracious, aren't I? That's considered a deadly sin for a Romano. I think I'll blame it on exhaustion." She took a deep breath and surprised him with a serene smile. "I'm sure this will be fine. Why don't I check out the kitchen and fix us some coffee?"

"I'll get it."

"In that case, I'll unpack our suitcases." Her smile turned teasing. "Maybe that'll give us more room to maneuver."

Considering the bags for their honeymoon trip had shown up in their bridal suite at the same time as their breakfast, their luggage fully packed and ready to go, he had no idea what they contained. "Let's hope whoever packed them for us threw in some swimsuits." And sleepwear that covered a bit more of Ariana than the night-gown she'd worn on their wedding night. Otherwise, he wouldn't survive the first night, let alone a full week.

While he prepared the coffee, Ariana unzipped the first suitcase. "Tons of casual wear and—hallelujah—a bathing suit."

After transferring the clothes from the suitcase to the dresser, she unearthed a sketch pad and pencils. He eyed it curiously as he offered her a lightly steaming mug. "Do you draw?"

"I do, yes." She accepted the mug and inhaled the fragrant scent of the coffee. Then she let out a low sigh of pleasure, one that wreaked havoc with his self-control. "What little talent I have, I inherited from my grandmother," she confessed.

He lifted an eyebrow in surprise. "Penelope?"

"Mmm. So what would you like to do first?" Her deliberate change of subject roused his curiosity, but he let it go for the time being. "After that flight, I wouldn't mind taking a short hike."

"Before jet lag hits?"

"Actually, my internal time clock will adjust faster than yours, since I'm now back in the same time zone as Italy."

"With all the traveling I've done for Dantes, I've discovered that a solid workout helps most." And maybe it would douse the tiny sparks of arousal that grew hotter and more pervasive the longer he remained cooped up in the cabin with her. "I'm up for a hike if you are. We can get a feel for the surroundings."

She smiled brightly. "Give me a second to change into a pair of shorts, and I'll be ready to go."

He worked them hard, following a trail that wound around the lake. At one point, he glanced over at Ariana. Realizing he was setting a blistering pace, he deliberately slowed down. It took her less than a dozen steps before she clued in. Throwing him a challenging look, she dashed ahead, her teasing laughter drifting back to him. He lagged behind, allowing her to build up a decent lead before pouring on the power. The instant she heard his footsteps pounding closer, she sped up.

She had glorious legs, long and toned and shapely. He quickly discovered just how she kept them in shape. She ran like she'd been born to do nothing else, moving with a supple grace. The ease with which she hurdled obstacles in their path would have done a gazelle proud. And as far as he was concerned, the view was spectacular. Not only did he get to admire her legs, but a gloriously rounded backside, as well.

He waited until they reached the final curve of the lake before overtaking her. The instant the dirt path turned to sand, he swooped in and snatched her high into his arms. Her shriek echoed across the lake, sending a brace of ducks airborne. He carried her a half dozen steps before flinging himself and his delectable armful into the shallows.

"How about a swim?" he suggested when she surfaced, sputtering.

For an instant, she simply stared at him. Then a laugh broke free. "You are insane."

Ariana flipped her hair back from her face, the dark length streaming down her back like an ebony waterfall. The bright sunlight reflected off the strands, catching in ruby highlights that Lazz had never noticed before. His gaze slipped lower, and the breath stopped dead in his lungs. She wore a thin, very wet, cotton shirt. The brilliant red clung to her upper torso, molding itself to generous breasts that were a fantasy come true.

He struggled to do the honorable thing and look away. But somehow his eyeballs had become disconnected from his brain. "Do me a favor, will you?" he asked politely.

She planted her hands on her hips. "You just threw me in the water, and now you want *me* to do *you* a favor?"

"Or not."

She relented with a smile. "What's the favor?"

"I seem to be having trouble controlling my caveman genes. Would you mind ducking down a little?"

Fate rewarded him with a few more seconds of visual bliss before comprehension set in. With a gasp, she sank downward so the water lapped around her shoulders. "Did your caveman genes enjoy the view?" she asked acerbically, her accent a bit more pronounced than before.

"They did. They really did."

She spared him a disgruntled look, one that took on an appreciative glint. "I must admit, my cavewoman genes are having some enjoyment, as well. Maybe too much enjoyment. If you don't mind, I think I'll go in and change."

He nodded. "Feel free."

She lifted an eyebrow in a manner as regal as it was pure Romano. "Would you mind turning around?"

"I'm afraid I would mind. But don't let that stop you."

Her mouth twitched and she splashed water at him. "You are a rotten man."

"Not rotten. But definitely all man."

He lunged at her, catching her around the waist and yanking her into his arms. He didn't give her time to catch her breath, let alone protest. He took her mouth in a kiss as thorough and urgent as the one they'd shared on their wedding night.

Her mouth was warm and wet and the most delicious thing he'd ever tasted. This time there weren't any witnesses to the embrace, and he could take his time and explore at his leisure. He half expected her to resist, to slap him or give him hell in Italian.

To his surprise, her curiosity matched his own. Her hands slipped upward to trace the contours of his face before sliding into his hair and tugging. But it wasn't a demand for release. It was a silent appeal for more.

With a harsh groan, he mated her mouth with his, deepening the kiss until their breath became one. His hands swept up and under her shirt and closed over her breasts. They were every bit as full and lush as they'd appeared through her wet shirt, the skin like velvet against his palms. The peaks turned to hard nubs beneath his touch, and he captured them between his fingers, torturing a moan of sheer pleasure from her.

For a tantalizing moment she pressed herself more fully into his embrace, giving with the soft want that was uniquely woman. Water swirled between them, carrying them together so their hips fit male to female. A groan snagged in his throat. It would be so easy to strip away the thin layers of clothing separating them and mate more than just their mouths. His hands swept downward, his thumbs hooking into the waistband of her shorts. Before he could slip them off her hips, she twisted free.

Wrapping her arms around herself, she dragged air into her lungs. "We shouldn't have done that," she informed him the instant she could speak.

"It was bound to happen, if only for curiosity's sake."

"Is your curiosity satisfied?"

"My curiosity's satisfied. But it hasn't done a damn thing for the rest of me."

"No, it hasn't done a damn thing for my rest, either." She slid her hands across her face as though to scrub the lingering traces of passion from it. "I would like to go inside and change. Would you mind staying here for a few minutes so I might have some privacy?"

"Of course."

He tormented himself a bit more by watching her wade from the lake before working off his libido with a long, hard swim. By the time he'd finished, all he could think about was food and sleep. Okay, he thought about Ariana, too. Most of all, he wondered how long it would take to talk her out of her first condition and into bed.

By the time he'd showered himself human again and changed into dry clothes, she had dinner prepared. "I'm not very good in the kitchen," she warned.

"That makes two of us."

She shrugged. "In that case, we'll take turns poisoning each other."

She'd done a reasonable job, punching up the canned soup with grated cheese, spinach, and roasted garlic. She'd also warmed up a loaf of bread and thrown together an olive oil and herb dipping sauce. Finally, she served them a salad topped with grilled chicken.

"I thought you said you didn't cook well," he commented as he polished off the last of the bread.

She lifted a shoulder. "You'll see. It's all downhill from here."

He grinned. "That's only because I fix dinner next."

"You know, I'm discovering you have a very nice sense of humor," she observed. "I like that about you. I worried during our negotiations because you were very…serious. Very autocratic."

His grin faded. "Having a sense of humor doesn't turn me into Marco."

"And I'm not Caitlyn." She shrugged again. "If we were honest, I think we'd both admit that we wouldn't want it otherwise. Even though my grandmother adored your brother, she was concerned that I might fall in love with him."

"I gather she didn't like that idea."

Ariana shook her head. "Not at all. She said he was all wrong for me. Charming, yes. A heart bigger than all of Italy, true. But he was missing something a husband should have."

"And what's that?" He couldn't have stopped the question if his life depended on it.

"She said a woman should only marry someone who has a clear sense of right and wrong and that sliver of gray that divides the two. In that sliver lies compassion, she always claimed. It was a quality my grandfather had. Before we left for Verdonia, she told me she saw that sliver in you."

He couldn't think of a higher compliment, though he

doubted Penelope would still be of that opinion if she knew the real reason he and Ariana had married. "I like the way your grandmother thinks." He tilted his head to one side. "How did she end up in a wheelchair?"

"It was from a car accident. She and my grandfather went over an embankment on a remote mountain road while touring Germany. They weren't located for two days. It was in all the newspapers at the time."

He stared, shocked. "My God."

"It was a hideous tragedy. My family kept the worst of the details from me, but I read copies of the reports on the Internet." It took her a moment to continue. "They said my grandfather was thrown clear of the car, but was badly injured. He died shortly before the rescuers found them. If they'd gotten there sooner, he'd have survived."

"And your grandmother?"

"She was trapped in the car. Her spine was damaged. She rarely speaks of the incident. I gather the only thing that kept her going was my grandfather. He couldn't get to her and she couldn't get to him, but they encouraged each other for those two days."

It made him see Penelope in an entirely new light. "How old were you when it happened?"

"Just a year."

"So, you don't remember your grandfather?"

"No."

He covered her hand with his. "I hope you'll find time to get to know Primo. I realize it won't be the same, but maybe you can get a feel for what it would have been like to have had a grandfather in your life."

Tears welled up in her eyes. "Thank you. I'd like that,

even if it's only temporary." She stood, strain showing on her face. "If you don't mind, I think I'll read for a little bit before turning in. It's been a long day."

"No problem."

Silence descended on the cabin as night fell. The temperature dropped, bringing a refreshing coolness. When he finally decided to turn in he discovered that Ariana had fallen asleep on the love seat. He debated picking her up and carrying her to bed. But he couldn't count on his self-control being strong enough to keep him from taking advantage of the situation. Stripping the blanket off the bed, he covered her with it. And then he turned away before he did something he'd regret.

The next several days passed in a similar manner. They ate, hiked, swam and threw fishing lines in the water. They told amusing stories about their family and discussed endless topics of interest. Lazz even managed to convince himself that their honeymoon getaway was spacious enough for two, though he noticed that they never stayed inside longer than absolutely necessary. Not while the bed remained the centerpiece of the cabin.

All the while they circled each other, pretending not to feel the sexual tension that grew with each passing hour of each passing day. It seemed to loom just over the horizon, like a storm rumbling in the distance. The worst hours were while he waited for Ariana to fall asleep on the love seat, hours during which he waged a private war to keep from scooping her up and putting an end to their stalemate.

Two days before they were scheduled to leave, he joined her on the stretch of imported sand by the lake.

She sat curled up on a towel, hard at work on her sketch pad. He handed her a bottle of ice-cold water.

"Do you mind?" he asked, inclining his head toward her sketch pad.

"Not at all." She handed it over, then cracked open the bottle and tilted back her head to take a long swallow of water.

Lazz forced himself to look away from that endless length of neck and the tantalizing curve of breast and focus on the drawings. There were page after page of them, mostly of the local flora and fauna. But his face had somehow found its way in there and in the most peculiar places. Peeking out from under a bush. In the spots of a fawn. On the tail of a fish. In the downy feathers of a duck. There was an irresistible whimsy to her art form that left him grinning.

"These are really outstanding. Very clever."

"Thanks."

"Have you ever thought of having a showing?"

She lifted a shoulder in a gesture that had become endearingly familiar over the past few days. "Not really."

"Would your family frown on it?"

"It's not that. It's just..." She made a face. "My drawings aren't to everyone's taste."

"Well, they're to *my* taste."

She held out her hand for her sketch pad. He started to pass it to her, but then surprised them both by taking her hand in his. The connection between them flared, hotter and stronger than ever before, mocking their efforts to keep it subdued. Lazz swore beneath his breath. He'd done everything he could to bury the attraction he felt, to keep it under control. But now it seemed to explode in great messy waves of need.

Ariana stiffened, as though sensing how close he'd come to the end of his restraint. "We can't," she whispered.

"Yes, we can. And yes, we will."

"You say that as though I have no choice in the matter."

"You have the choice of when and where. But this is going to happen. You know it. You just haven't reconciled yourself to it yet."

She snatched up her sketch pad and pencil. "We only have two more days, Lazz. We can hold out that long."

"Possibly. But then what?" he pressed. "What happens when we return to San Francisco?"

"We'll have more room." She shot a frustrated glance at the cabin. "We won't be living on top of each other like we are here. We can go our separate ways."

"And at night? When we're lying in bed filled with want?"

She shuddered, and he could see her teetering, poised on the verge of tumbling. With an exclamation of frustration, she tossed aside the bottle of water and shot to her feet. "I'm going for a walk."

He slowly stood. "You do that." He pulled one of the cell phones from his pocket and tossed it to her. "But I'll still be here when you return. And so will that bed."

Without a word, she spun on her heel and walked away. But this time she looked back. This time he saw the coming surrender.

Lazz checked his watch for the umpteenth time. Damn it. Ariana had been gone for hours, and a call had just come through warning of an impending storm. He shot an uneasy glance toward the sky. Threatening clouds gathered with unnerving speed, descending on the peaks of the surrounding mountains in a great, boiling mass, like an army preparing to sweep down and invade the valley below. Lightning shot through the bruise-colored center of the storm mass.

He reached for the cell phone that was a mate to Ariana's and punched in her number again. The last half dozen times he'd tried, the call hadn't gone through. No doubt it had something to do with the approaching storm. This time, he was in luck. The call connected.

"Lazz?" he heard Ariana's voice say. He also realized she was speaking in Italian, a dead giveaway as to her emotional state. He could barely hear her through the static. But what he did hear had his blood turning to ice. "I'm lost."

He spoke swiftly, not sure how long the connection would last. "What direction were you heading when you left?"

"Along the stream away from the cabin. After a while there was a path that cut off to the right. There were these really gorgeous purplish-blue flowers. I wanted to sketch them. I just kept following the flowers. Then I fell down an incline and twisted my ankle. When I climbed back out I couldn't find the flowers or the path or the stream or anything."

He could hear the incipient thread of panic weaving through her voice. "Leave your cell phone on," he instructed. "I'll call Tolken and see if he can get a GPS lock on—"

The connection cut out and Lazz swore. No signal

and no time. He needed to find Ariana and fast. First things first. If she'd twisted her ankle he'd have to wrap it. Some food and water would be helpful if they were caught out in the storm. He could use one of the backpacks he'd noticed in the boathouse, along with a couple of the rain slickers stored there. She'd also be cold from either fear or shock, so a sweater wouldn't be a bad idea. Five minutes later he had everything he needed, including a pair of flashlights and a compass.

Jogging around the lake, he hit the trail that paralleled the stream just as the first boom of thunder rumbled down the hillside like cannon fire. He picked up his pace, keeping a sharp eye out for the path Ariana had indicated. He found it less than a mile along. The flowers she'd described trembled beneath a gust of rain-laden wind, but he paused long enough to check his compass before continuing on. He took off again, watching the path for any section that tumbled down a hillside. Unfortunately, since they were in the mountains, there were endless drop-offs.

A quick glance behind warned that the storm would break soon. The sky turned nighttime dark, and a curtain of rain cut him off from where he'd left the path along the stream. The curtain marched steadily in his direction. He continued onward, calling Ariana's name as he went.

Five minutes farther along he came across a grassy expanse covered in a colorful banquet of flowers. On the far side of the area, the grass ended abruptly in a steep bank, where dirt and rocks mixed with uprooted flowers cascaded into a deep ravine. There wasn't a doubt in his mind that his wife had slid down the hillside into that dark pocket. He couldn't say how he knew; he simply did.

"Ariana? Can you hear me?"

Overhead the storm broke, rain slamming against the ground so hard he couldn't hear his own voice, let alone any response from Ariana. Cautiously, he climbed down into the ravine, slipping and sliding as the rain turned the dirt to an avalanche of mud. The instant he reached the bottom, his awareness of her grew stronger, along with the certainty that she'd been here not too long ago. He shone the flashlight around until he found the proof he needed, the spot where she must have landed. Part of a snapped pencil rested on top of a broken boulder, and the torn remnants of her sketch pad blew toward a narrow channel of water that cut the ravine in two.

After rescuing the sketch pad, he carefully circled the area a second time until he spotted where she'd climbed back out of the gully. Unfortunately, it was on the opposite side from where she'd fallen in, which explained why she'd been unable to find her way back to the stream.

He followed in Ariana's footsteps. Below him, the ravine rapidly filled with water, the narrow channel that bisected the ravine becoming a churning river of mud, rock and mountain runoff. Worse, the rain was turning the loose dirt beneath his hands and feet into a mudslide that threatened to send him right back down the hillside. He had no idea how long it took him to work his way to the top. By the time he hauled himself over the ridge, he was up to his eyeballs in mud and soaked to the skin, despite his rain gear.

"Ariana?" he shouted. She was close. He could feel her now. Hell, he could practically taste her.

Above the sound of the rain, he heard her faint cry. "Here! I'm over here."

The beam from his flashlight cut through the gloom and landed on her. His wife sat huddled at the base of a towering pine, her knees drawn tight to her chest and her arms wrapped around her legs. He broke into a run. When he reached her side, he didn't say a word. He simply pulled her into his arms and kissed her.

Five

From: Lazzaro_Dante@DantesJewelry.com
Date: 2008, August 05 10:34 PDST
To: Bambolina@fornitore.it
Subject: Marriage Contract, Premarital Conditions...
Next
Now that we've dealt with the public aspects of our
marriage, perhaps we should deal with the private.
Condition #4: No intermingling. We'll keep our
private lives separate on all levels...financial,
physical, social, etc.
L.

From: Bambolina@fornitore.it
Date: 2008, August 05 19:59 CEST
To: Lazzaro_Dante@DantesJewelry.com

Subject: Re: Marriage Contract, Premarital Conditions...Next

I actually had to look up the word *intermingling*. Okay, okay. I get it. In public we are joined hips to lips. And in private, my high heels stay out of your closet. Ciao! Ariana

One second Ariana's mouth was cold and wet and the next it turned to liquid warmth. Lazz sank inward, driven to tell her without words everything he felt. Traces of his fear and concern made the kiss hard and urgent. He forked his hands into her damp hair while she met him kiss for kiss, the need for reassurance unrelenting.

Minutes slid by and the tenor changed, the embrace easing into a joyful mating. His relief at finding her alive and relatively unhurt blunted the edginess from moments before. It grew softer, gentler, as he drank his fill. Until passion pushed the kiss back into the danger zone.

The sharp crack of thunder and an answering sizzle of lightning brought him to his senses. Reluctantly, Lazz drew back. "Sit tight."

"Trust me, I'm not going anywhere."

Stripping off his slicker, he spread it across the branches directly above Ariana to provide some protection from the rain. He ducked beneath the temporary canopy and crouched beside her.

"How are you holding up?"

"I'm cold. Scared. I hurt my ankle when I fell. But other than that, I'm fine." Her eyes were huge and dark in her pale face, and her gaze clung to his, practically eating him alive. "Better now that you're here."

"Let's see what we can do to fix you up." He opened

his backpack and pulled out the sweater and the extra slicker he'd brought for her. Helping her to her feet, he spread the slicker on the wet ground directly under their makeshift canopy. "Take off your shirt."

To his surprise, she didn't question him, let alone protest. She simple grabbed the hem of her shirt and yanked it over her head and off. Without waiting for him to suggest it, she also removed her bra before taking the sweater and pulling it on. He had enough time—and was still male enough, despite the circumstances—to admire the beauty of her shape and to realize that reality far exceeded what he'd seen up to this point.

She sighed in pleasure. "I didn't think I'd ever get warm again."

"Enjoy it while it lasts. It's a long hike back to the cabin."

"Especially with my ankle the way it is." Taking the hand he offered, she resumed her seat beneath the tree. "I can't believe you found me."

"I have a feeling finding you was the easy part." He glanced over his shoulder. "We can't go back the way we came. The ravine's filling up with water."

"Is there another path we can take?"

"Let's hope so. I've got a fairly good idea which direction we need to go."

"That's an excellent start."

He settled down beside her and grinned. "I like your confidence." He dipped into the backpack again and pulled out a bottle of water and a candy bar. "Have something to eat and drink while I check your ankle."

To his amusement, she devoured the chocolate with unmistakable greed, even licking her fingers to make certain she consumed every last morsel. While she sipped the water, he examined her ankle. Some nasty bruising and swelling, he decided, but not broken, thank God. And not as bad as he feared, though bad enough that it would make for a long and difficult return trip.

He dug into the backpack again and pulled out the bandage he'd unearthed in the emergency kit at the cabin. "I'm going to wrap your ankle with your shoe on to give it some extra support."

"Good idea." She flinched as thunder crashed over-head. "The storm's getting worse, isn't it?"

"A little."

"Is it safe to move?"

"Not for a bit." He finished wrapping her foot and settled in next to her. "We're in a pocket between two hillsides, under a stand of fairly short trees. Sitting here is better than being out in the open. I want to wait until the storm moves off a little and then see if we can't make it back to the cabin before nightfall."

She capped the water and handed it back to him. "Thank you for coming to find me."

Did she think he wouldn't? He tucked her close to help warm her up. "You're my wife."

"Not really."

His mouth tightened. "You're my wife," he re-peated, more strongly this time. "I wouldn't leave you out alone in this."

Ariana fell silent for a few minutes. Then she said, "I could feel you, you know. I could feel you coming for me."

Just as he'd felt her. Lazz didn't want to admit that

what he considered instinct might have been enhanced by something else. Something more. Something that caused his palm to itch and desire to cling to him like a second skin. Something that made him want to sweep her into his arms and carry her to safety. To strip off her clothes and warm her with his touch. To complete what remained incomplete between them.

"You must have heard me," he attempted to explain away her reaction. "Or seen the flashlight beam."

She continued as though he'd never spoken. "I was afraid and alone. And then I sensed you coming, and the fear and loneliness melted away. I knew that if I just waited a few more minutes you'd find me. And you did."

He wanted to deny her words, to deny the suggestion that whatever connected them might be The Inferno. The Inferno was a lie, the proof of that lie evident in his own parents' marriage. His brothers might have been deluded into believing, into creating romantic fantasies out of plain, old-fashioned lust, but he was the most pragmatic of all the Dantes and he refused—*refused*—to allow his life to be controlled or dictated by a fantasy that could vanish as quickly as it had appeared.

"You gave excellent directions, Ariana. It wasn't hard to find you. In fact, if you hadn't gotten turned around when you fell into that ravine, you'd have found your own way back to the cabin. It was just bad luck."

"Did you love her very much?" She waited a heartbeat before adding, "Caitlyn. Is that why you don't believe me?"

"Caitlyn is Marco's wife."

"That doesn't answer my question."

"No, I didn't love her. Not really. Not the way Marco did." He forced himself to admit the truth. "And not the way Caitlyn loves Marco."

"But you believed she was your Inferno match, even if for a short time. You said you felt something for her once."

He dismissed Ariana's comment with a restless shrug. "Yes, I felt something. And I deluded myself into thinking it might be The Inferno and that she might be responsible. I was wrong."

"You told me it happened in Marco's conference room, the morning after they were married. The day I was there with my father," she added pointedly.

"Yes."

"But you still don't believe in The Inferno, do you? You refuse to consider that maybe what you felt was for me and not Caitlyn."

"I don't believe, Ariana." Thunder underscored his response. He continued to look at her, so she could read the truth in his gaze. "I never have and I never will."

"You must sense something," she insisted. "I can't be the only one of us experiencing whatever this is."

"It's simple desire. We're physically attracted to each other. We're two people—two *married* people—confined in a limited space. To make matters more difficult, we made sex a condition of our marriage."

Her lush mouth twisted into a wry, self-deprecating smile. "I believe I made *no* sex a condition of our marriage."

"Am I sensing regret?"

Lightning sizzled from the sky, striking close enough to fill the air with a sharp, metallic scent. He felt rather than heard Ariana's swift inhalation. And then she curled into him, burying her face against his shoulder.

"Yes, you sense regret," came her muffled voice. "I regret every last one of those ridiculous conditions we agreed to. I regret not having met you instead of Marco all those months ago. I regret that our parents ever signed that hideous contract. I regret that the first time we touched, the first time we kissed, was standing at the altar on our wedding day."

"I couldn't agree more." Lazz held her close, wrapping himself around her so she stayed safe and warm. "I've always wondered why Dad drafted that contract. Do you have any idea?"

"None. If my father knows, he hasn't said."

"I find it odd that Vittorio agreed to Dad's proposition. Was it just the money?"

She winced. "I'm sure that was part of it." Pain bled into the words, and he realized that on some level she must feel as though her father had betrayed her, allowing avarice to outweigh his love for his daughter. "He said it was something your father told him that finally convinced him to sign, but he refused to explain what. He claimed it wasn't the right time."

Lightning flashed in the distance, and the thunder took a moment to rumble a response. Though the rain remained steady, it didn't pound the ground the way it had only moments before. A deep gray seeped into the hillside, warning of the advent of dusk. Lazz stood and stripped the slicker off the branches above them. Shaking it out, he passed it down to Ariana.

"Here, put this on."

"Are we leaving?" she asked in relief.

"We're going to give it a shot." He checked his compass. "I'm hoping we can parallel the path on the other side of the ravine. The stream shouldn't be too far along. Once we find that, we'll be back to the cabin in no time."

After donning the slicker they'd been sitting on, he searched the underbrush for a sturdy branch Ariana could use as a walking stick. Then he slung the backpack over one shoulder while bracing his wife with the other. It had taken him a mere five minutes to traverse the distance from the stream to the ravine. Returning to that spot took a full thirty.

Pain and weariness lined Ariana's face as they rested on a mossy boulder near the stream. "I would never have made it without you. Thank you." She regarded the stone-strewn path ahead of them, and her chin set into a determined line. "What do you say we tackle this next part before it gets any darker?"

"I'd say you were pretty damn amazing, Mrs. Dante." He dug in his backpack for another candy bar and handed it to her. "Eat this first, and then we'll push off."

It took them two more hours to reach the cabin. Ariana's legs buckled mere steps from the porch, and Lazz swung her into his arms. "Just another minute," he reassured, "and I'll have you in a nice hot tub."

She moaned in response. "Who knew I'd want to be any wetter than I already am. But a hot bath…"

He shoved open the front door and carried her inside. "With bubbles."

"Stop. You're killing me."

He reached for the light switch and flicked it on.

Nothing happened. "Hell. It just figures." He gently set Ariana down, helping her balance on her one good foot. "Looks like the storm knocked out the power."

"No bath?" she asked with surprising equanimity.

"There should be enough hot water," he reassured. "And as soon as I get the generator going, there'll be more than enough."

Using his flashlight to guide him, Lazz carried her through to the bathroom and turned on the faucet. Sure enough, hot water came pouring out. He upended a jar of bath crystals, watching with interest as they exploded into bubbles. Then he shone the beam of light in Ariana's direction. She stood awkwardly on one leg, laughter dancing in her dark eyes.

"Too much bubble?"

"A bit," she conceded.

"Do you need help getting in?"

"You sound entirely too hopeful." She shook her head. "If you'd leave me one of the flashlights, I should be fine."

"I can do better than that." He shone the light toward a trio of squat candles grouped on the tile ledge that surrounded the tub. "Will that do?"

Her sigh of pleasure was answer enough. "Perfect."

He left her to it while he powered up the generator. To his relief, it started with ease. Finally, he went to the freezer and removed a bag of frozen corn, poured two glasses of wine and returned to the bathroom. He paused outside the door.

"Cover up with bubbles. I'm coming in." He heard a feminine yelp, followed by a soft splash. Grinning, he pushed open the door. "Hope you don't mind."

"I do, as a matter of fact."

"Maybe this will help." He handed her the wine. "Rest your ankle on the edge of the tub."

"Corn?"

"Frozen corn." Draping it across her ankle, he headed for the shower stall and began to strip.

"What are you doing now?" Nervousness cascaded through her voice. She glanced over her shoulder and then whipped around again. "You're taking your clothes off."

"True." He paused deliberately. "I'm wet, filthy and tired. I'm taking a shower, assuming there's any hot water left. And if there's not, I'll be wet, cold and tired. But at least I'll be clean."

"Yes, of course," she murmured in Italian. "I wasn't thinking."

He smiled. Did she have any idea how much she gave away when she switched languages? "I could always join you in the tub," he suggested.

"Or not."

"There are enough bubbles in there for two. And considering the size of that thing, there's more than enough room for both of us."

She sank lower in the tub. "You choose the oddest times to display your sense of humor."

"Huh. I could have sworn I was being dead serious."

He turned on the shower and braced himself. To his relief, it wasn't as bad as he feared. Lukewarm, at best, but the illusion of warmth lasted long enough for him to scrub down. Once he'd dried off, he regarded his wife. Only the top of her head was visible above the dissipating layer of bubbles, not to mention one shapely leg.

He grabbed a stack of towels and piled them within reach of the tub. "I'm going to start a fire. Are you okay?"

"I'm fine. Thank you, Lazz."

She'd switched back to English, and when she glanced up, she managed to regard him with the sort of regal poise that must have been drummed into her from infancy. And yet, he could feel the want sizzling behind the facade.

Something had changed as a result of what they'd gone through during the storm. They'd come out the other side and everything had been different. There'd always been a strong, sexual awareness between them—not The Inferno. Not a chance. But definitely an awareness. Now, that awareness had sharpened to a keen edge. One that was going to cut them if they didn't do something to blunt it.

"Call me if you need help getting out." He paused at the door and shot her a wicked grin, one he hoped disguised how he really felt. "Looks like I should have used more bubble bath, not less."

Ariana glanced down and gasped. Embarrassing gaps had appeared in the bubbles. The tips of her breasts peeked through one of those gaps, while the curve of her hip and belly could clearly be seen through another.

She shivered despite the warmth of the water. Humorous remarks aside, she'd never seen that look in Lazz's eyes before. Sure, she'd seen awareness. Desire. But not to this extent. Not that bone-deep hunger that had turned his eyes to jade. He wanted her. Badly. It showed in the tautness of his face and the ferocity of his gaze, as well as the rigid play of muscles across his impressive chest. It suggested a man hovering on the edge, clawing to hold himself in check.

This time she shivered for real. The bathwater had gone from toasty to cool, and the bubbles were little more than a delicious memory. Even the bag of frozen corn had turned warm and soggy.

Levering herself onto the edge of the platform surrounding the tub, she grabbed a towel for her hair and wrapped a second one around herself. Her ankle felt better, at least enough for her to hobble out of the bathroom in search of clean clothes. The central portion of the cabin remained in darkness with only the flickering light from the fireplace to pierce the shadows.

Lazz stood as she limped into the room. "You should have called me."

"I managed."

"Do you need help dressing?"

Absolutely not. "I don't think so, thanks."

He moved from his stance by the fireplace, and she lost him in the darkness, tracking him by voice alone. "I'll go top off the generator while you change. Feel free to turn on a light if you want. I left them off to conserve fuel so we could keep the refrigerator and freezer running."

She offered a self-conscious smile. "Not to mention the hot water heater."

There was a stillness about him that unnerved her. A purposefulness. And she could practically taste the tension thickening the air. "That, too."

She clung to the edges of her damp towel. She couldn't remember the last time she'd felt this awkward. Lazz must have sensed as much because he left the cabin without another word. Ariana didn't waste any time. She limped to the dresser as quickly as her ankle would allow and dug through the drawers. She yanked out clothing at random, anything that would give her adequate coverage.

She'd just finished dressing when an unearthly screech split the air, followed by a boom so violent it jolted the cabin right down to its foundations and literally knocked her off her feet. She lay on the floor, fighting for breath, not daring to move. Whatever just happened, it had killed the generator.

The instant the thought entered her mind, she bolted upright and shrieked, "Lazz!"

She scrambled to her feet and hobbled to the back door of the cabin. Turning the knob, she attempted to open it, but it wouldn't budge no matter how hard she shoved. She threw her full weight against it, horrified when her actions made absolutely no impact. Something had wedged the door shut. She hammered on the wooden surface and shouted for Lazz, panic sweeping through her.

He was out there. Whatever had caused that hideous noise and knocked out the generator, Lazz had been there when it had happened. The flashlight. Where had she put her flashlight? She stumbled back toward the fireplace and found it on the table that fronted the love seat. Switching it on, she hurried to the front door and threw it open. The storm had circled back on itself and continued unabated, lashing the clearing and forest with wind and rain. Thunder rumbled, the rolling boom a far different sound than the one that had knocked her off her feet. Lightning forked a jagged path across the sky, and that's when she saw him.

Lazz came toward her through the rain, tall and broad and—as far as she could tell—undamaged. Ignoring the stab of pain from her ankle, Ariana shot across the porch, down the steps and into the storm. He broke into a run as she made a beeline for him. The next instant, he scooped her up into his arms.

"Are you all right?" he demanded, urgency underscoring the question.

"Fine. I'm fine. What about you?" Her hands raced over his face and down across the breadth of his shoulders, searching for any signs of injury. "Are you hurt?"

"Nothing serious." He hustled toward the porch. "Though it was a close call."

She knew she was crying, but hoped he attributed it to rain instead of tears. "What happened? What made that horrible sound?"

"Tree came down. Took out the generator shed a few seconds before I got there."

The tears came faster. "It didn't hit you? You're sure you're not hurt?"

His arms tightened around her, holding her snug against his heart. She could feel the calming beat, the steady reassurance that he'd survived and was here with her, safe and sound. "I got brushed back by a few of the smaller branches. Nothing serious. But the tree blocked off the back of the cabin."

He carried her across the threshold and inside. The symbolism of his actions didn't strike her until much, much later. "Show me. Show me this 'nothing serious.'" Struggling free of his hold, she shoved at his jacket, tugging it off his shoulders, not even aware of her actions. "Show me where you were hit," she demanded.

He didn't fight her. He must have understood her fear and concern. "Across the shoulder. Right arm."

"Take off your shirt. Let me see." She aimed the flashlight at his torso and waited. When he didn't immediately move to comply, she added, "I'm serious, Lazz. Do it."

He gripped the bottom of his shirt and whipped it up and off. For some reason, he focused on a point over her shoulder, almost as though standing there before her, stripped to the waist, had left him vulnerable on some level. She understood the feeling all too well, considering that not an hour ago their positions had been reversed. Now it was her turn to care for him.

It took her a moment to regain her focus. She'd seen him bare chested any number of times. It still had the power to steal her breath away. Heaven help her but he was built. His jeans rode low on narrow hips, offering her plenty of viewing room.

Strong, lean muscle rippled across the endless expanse of golden skin, begging for her touch. Soft against hard. Gentle overlaying power. She felt the piercing siren's call of The Inferno—*no, not The Inferno.* Lazz had insisted it was lust, nothing more. No matter how she might long for it to be different, their feelings for one another weren't the stuff of legend.

Ariana forced herself to put aside foolish dreams and examine Lazz for any signs of injury. She found evidence almost immediately. Several gouges streaked across his shoulder and down his chest, while a bruise was already forming across his right bicep.

The beam from the flashlight trembled. "You *were* hurt."

He glanced down and shrugged. "It's nothing. Just a scratch."

Tentatively, she reached for him, stroking his chest with trembling fingertips. The instant she touched him, he froze. A harsh sound rumbled in his throat, and he closed his eyes. A tense second passed. And then he looked at her again, and she realized that he'd lost the battle to hold himself in check. Gently, he reached for her. And just as gently, she surrendered.

Six

From: Bambolina@fornitore.it
Date: 2008, August 05 22:08 CEST
To: Lazzaro_Dante@DantesJewelry.com
Subject: Marriage Contract, Premarital Conditions…
My turn ;)
Lazz, I'm a little concerned about how we will eventually end our marriage. Romanos don't believe in divorce, and I have no intention of becoming the first to change that.
Counter-Condition #2: I would like to have our marriage annulled when the time comes.
Ciao! Ariana

From: Lazzaro_Dante@DantesJewelry.com
Date: 2008, August 05 14:36 PDST

To: Bambolina@fornitore.it
Subject: Re: Marriage Contract, Premarital Condi-
tions...My turn ;)
Is this open for negotiation?
L.

From: Bambolina@fornitore.it
Date: 2008, August 06 00:19 CEST
To: Lazzaro_Dante@DantesJewelry.com
Subject: Re: Marriage Contract, Premarital Condi-
tions...My turn ;)
Not even a little.

Lazz cupped Ariana's hips and locked her against him, a delicious slide of male against female. Before she could do more than catch her breath in a soft gasp, he slid under her shirt and upward until he hit hot, satiny skin.

"I've tried." His voice contained the same raw, gritty quality as sandpaper. "I've done my best to leave you alone. But I can't. If you still want me to honor your request, you need to say so. Now. While I can still stop what's about to happen."

Common sense struggled to override base desire. Her motives for refusing to make love to her husband were sound. They were part of her core values, as vital to her well-being as her heartbeat. In addition, Brimstone was missing. How would Lazz view her actions tonight if her father was unable to recover the stone?

It didn't take any consideration at all. He'd be furious and might even wonder if she'd sacrificed herself on the altar, as it were, in order to protect her family. But in this moment, her need to complete the bond between them overrode every last sensible thought. Whatever connection had formed when they stood before the altar and first joined hands had slipped into her heart and soul and become as much a part of her as those values.

As hard as she tried to resist, she'd have an easier time convincing the tide not to turn or the sun to dim its flames. She wanted him. Wanted his hands on her. Wanted their clothes off. "Don't stop. Please, Lazz. Make love to me."

He shook his head, regret reflected in his expression. "I don't think I know how to love." He swept her up into his arms once again and carried her to the bed. He settled her onto the mattress and followed her down. "But you make me want to try. And I swear what I feel for you is unlike anything I've ever felt before."

He didn't give her time to respond, but lowered his head and took her mouth in a kiss so tender, so warm and life-affirming that any remaining resistance slipped away. She opened to him, welcoming him inward.

A delicious humming darted through her veins. "More," she murmured.

"Anything you want."

"You. I just want you."

He reached for her, then hesitated at the last minute. "I just realized. I have no way of protecting you."

She stared blankly. "Protecting me?"

"From pregnancy," he clarified.

She struggled to think straight, to admit—even to herself—that she'd considered that possibility over the course of the past week, despite her marital conditions. That she'd done the mental arithmetic…just in case. "It's safe."

He accepted her at her word. "Thank heaven for small miracles."

He grasped the hem of her cotton shirt and drew it up and over her head. She emerged breathless and rumpled. Lightning burned the room in hard white light, spotlighting her partial nudity. She heard Lazz's sharp inhalation and caught a glimpse of the undisguised desire that cut sharp grooves on either side of his mouth. Green and gold fire flashed in his eyes as he looked at her, igniting a scorching path across her skin.

Darkness consumed them once again, alleviated only by the banked glow emanating from the fireplace. Thunder rattled the windows, but this time she didn't flinch at the sound, not while Lazz held her safe within the protective warmth of his arms. His hands glided across the silken curve of her abdomen and upward to cup her breast.

Her heartbeat stuttered before catching and echoing the beat of his, and frantic need exploded deep in the pit of her stomach. She arched farther into his embrace, a low moan disturbing the air between them.

"I've never touched anything so soft," he murmured. "Or so warm."

"I think I'm melting into the mattress."

He chuckled, the sound deliciously intimate. "That makes two of us. It's either melt, or set the sheets on fire."

"Yes, please."

"I'll get right on that."

And he did. He caught her nipple between his teeth and tugged. She didn't have a hope of concealing her response, not when it shuddered through her. He absorbed her reaction and excited another as he followed a velveteen path downward.

The breath escaped her lungs in a desperate rush. "What are you doing?"

He paused, tracing the indent of her belly with his mouth and then with his tongue. "You can't say that in English, can you?"

She groaned. "No. Please, Lazz."

"Let me in, Ariana. I want to know every part of you."

"Don't. I can't—"

Reason fled and so did any capacity to speak. He slid his hands beneath her backside and lifted her. He touched her with surprising delicacy, a slow, thorough exploration that had her clutching fistfuls of the sheet beneath them. Her thighs tensed as he delved into the damp heat of her, and she would have jackknifed off the bed if he hadn't held her in place. Again he touched her, the tip of his tongue skating ruthlessly along its predetermined path.

The muscles in her belly drew taut, and she literally lost the ability to see or hear or reason. A deep quaking struck, the epicenter just beneath his tongue and radiating outward in great, rolling waves. She'd never experienced anything like it before, couldn't seem to process what he'd done to her.

But he wasn't finished. Before the aftermath of the final quake had fully died away, he surged upward and sank into her with a single, unerring stroke. She froze at the unexpected pain and fullness, catching her lip between her teeth so she wouldn't cry out.

"What's wrong?"

She took a deep, careful breath. "It's a bit uncomfortable," she admitted.

"I assume it's been a while?"

"A while," she confirmed. "If never is a while."

"Never?" A moment of stunned silence followed. "Are you telling me you've never made love before?" he asked carefully.

Did he even realize he referred to it as lovemaking? Until that moment he'd always called it sex. "No, I've never made love before. I once heard some friends of Constantine's—ex-friends—taking bets to see who could relieve me of my virginity first."

"Bastards."

She shrugged. "It was because I'm a Romano. It would have given them bragging rights to have been the first. But perhaps I should have mentioned it to you sooner."

He rested his forehead against hers. "That might have been a good idea."

"Has this deflated your interest?" she asked politely.

A rough laugh escaped him. "Not even a little. I almost wish it had."

"It shouldn't be a problem if you go slowly."

"Give me a minute and I'll see what I can do. Right now, it's taking all my self-control not to move."

"What if I move?" Cautiously, she arched upward, absorbing a bit more of him, before sinking back down again. "How's that?"

He groaned. "Yes."

"More?"

He didn't answer. He simply took her mouth with his. His tongue slid inward before withdrawing in a leisurely rhythm. Understanding what he wanted, she shifted her hips upward, matching stroke for stroke. Little by little the rhythm picked up, increasing in speed and depth until she'd fully sheathed him.

She couldn't say when he joined the dance. One moment she was leading, and the next they matched each other move for move. Scorching heat slicked across her skin and sank into her pores, radiating through her. She could feel the quickening approach again and moved to chase it.

Lazz raced with her, encouraging her with word and touch. Then he was driving their movements, driving her. They climbed, fast and hard, teetering breathlessly at the very peak. The air exploded from her in a sharp cry and she felt his final push to join her as she tumbled over. He stiffened within her embrace, frozen for a timeless moment.

She'd never seen anything more soul-shattering than his expression in that intensely personal moment. She'd brought him to this. It showed in his eyes, a knowledge that whatever connected them was utterly unique and all-consuming. That her touch, her embrace, had fulfilled him in ways he'd never experienced before. That no matter who or what had come before, she had changed him.

As though aware of how much he'd given away, he closed his eyes. "I'm sorry, Ariana."

"Sorry?" She stared in bewilderment. "Why are you sorry?"

"You deserve more than I can give you." The admission was torn from him. "Your first time should have been with someone you loved."

"How do you know it wasn't?"

A muscle jerked in his jaw. "Love doesn't guarantee a happily-ever-after marriage. It didn't for my parents. In fact, they set a spectacular example of love gone wrong. I'd rather not follow in their footsteps. I'd rather not build our relationship into some ridiculous fantasy. Because when the fall comes, it's going to be long and hard."

"What about your grandparents?" she protested. "Your brothers? Haven't they shown that a marriage can endure? That love can, as well?"

"It's early days for my brothers. And my grandparents are merely the exception that proves the rule." He took her hand in his as he rolled off of her. She doubted he was even aware of the way he interlaced their fingers so their palms were joined. "Right before my father died, I remember him telling me how alike we were. That I got my logical bent from him and that it would make a successful marriage more difficult for me than my brothers."

"And you think that means you can't love?" she asked, stunned.

"I think it means he discovered The Inferno wasn't real. He didn't believe in it any more than I do. I think he was telling me that it didn't exist, no matter what Primo claimed to the contrary. That I shouldn't go looking for what couldn't be found."

She stared, appalled. "Did your father actually say that?"

Lazz's mouth twisted. "Not in so many words. But I'm logical, which makes me fairly good at connecting the dots." He released her hand and cupped her face. "Do you realize you speak in Italian whenever you're upset?"

"Like now?"

"Like now." He traced a fingertip from the hollow of her throat to the tip of her breast. "Of course, you also speak Italian when you're aroused."

Her eyes fluttered shut. "Like now?"

"Oh, yeah."

She slid into helpless surrender, enjoying the delicious give of female to male. "This wasn't supposed to happen. And it's definitely not supposed to happen again."

"It was inevitable."

"You don't understand."

"I understand perfectly. You don't believe in divorce, and I don't believe in love." He feathered a kiss across her mouth. And then another. "So where does that leave us, Ariana? Do you want to change the conditions we agreed to?"

A bittersweet laugh escaped her. "In case you didn't notice, the conditions have already been changed."

Lazz conceded her point with a brief smile. "What do you want from me?"

Love. A home. A real marriage, she wanted to say. But he wasn't capable of providing any of those things. "I'm not asking you for anything."

"Aren't you?"

She flinched. Was she so easy to read? Could he really see into her heart, see the dreams and hopes she kept safely tucked away there? Had she left herself so open and vulnerable? One careless touch and he could shatter all she held most dear. Assuming he hadn't already. She needed to protect herself and pull back before he hurt her more than he had already. At the very least she needed to pull back until her father had found Brimstone. Because if Lazz ever found out that she'd known it was missing and had still gone through with their wedding, he'd never forgive the betrayal. Not after what Caitlyn and Marco had done to him.

She slid from his embrace and escaped the bed. Snatching up the sheet, she wound it around herself. "This—" She gestured toward the rumpled bed. "We need to agree that our sexual encounter never occurred."

He raised an eyebrow. "Sexual encounter?"

Her chin shot up. "Would you prefer I call it love-making?"

"Touché." He lifted onto an elbow, not in the least concerned about his nudity, and regarded her through narrowed eyes. "You think we can just pretend tonight never happened?"

She kicked the trailing end of the sheet to one side. "Yes."

"And if we pretend hard enough, we can have our marriage annulled?" he asked in a neutral voice.

Pain filled her, a soul-deep ache. "I don't know."

He hesitated. "We don't have to annul it. Or divorce. There's a third option."

She froze. "What do you mean?"

"I mean we can stay married."

"Because I was a virgin? Because we had sex?"

He shook his head. "Just because I don't believe in love doesn't mean that I don't believe in marriage. I want to have children someday."

She drew in a sharp breath. Did he have any idea

how insulting she found his offer? "And since we find each other physically compatible, why not?"

"That was more than physical compatibility. Way more."

"So, I'll do? Physically, intellectually, socially, I meet all the criteria for a wife?"

He swore. "I'm suggesting we consider turning our marriage into something more than what we originally discussed. If you're not interested—"

"No. I'm not."

Not on his terms. Not in such a cold-blooded, *logical* fashion. She closed her eyes, fighting tears. Was he really so emotionally detached that he didn't understand how his "suggestion" came across? That he didn't see how she ached for him to consider the possibility—even if for one tiny second—that fantasy could become reality? That his Dante family legacy might be alive and well and burning within them both?

She gathered up the shreds of her self-control. "Here's what we're going to do. Since the generator shed has been smashed, first thing in the morning we're going to call Tolken and ask to be flown out of here. Then we're returning home. When we get back to San Francisco, you're going to go your way and I'm going mine."

He climbed off the bed and stood before her in all his glory. She struggled not to look, but couldn't seem to help herself. He had the most magnificent body she'd ever seen. And for a short time it had been hers to touch and taste and take deep inside herself.

It didn't seem to matter that they were worlds apart emotionally. It didn't dim the want. Desire still hammered away at her, tempting her to bend. To give. To tumble again into an embrace she wanted more than anything, even though it promised nothing in return. At least, nothing permanent.

"You're right," he surprised her by saying. "First thing in the morning we are leaving. But when we return to San Francisco your way is the same as mine. You made a commitment to me and you will honor it."

"And you promised not to touch me," she shot back. "It looks like we were both disappointed."

Instead of rousing his anger, her comment provoked a laugh. "You gave me permission to break that agreement. And I wasn't the least disappointed." He took a step closer. And then he did something totally unfair. He swept his hand along the side of her face. Just that. Just that single touch. So gentle. So tender. Sincere regret darkened his eyes. "But I'm sorry if you were, especially considering it was your first time. I'd like to change that, if you'll let me."

She stared at him in desperate silence. She couldn't have answered him if her life depended on it. Her first time hadn't been a disappointment. Far from it. It had been the most incredible night in her life, one she wanted to relive as often as possible. But that would mean surrendering. And surrender meant heartache.

"Tell me, sweetheart. Tell me what you want." He reached for the sheet and loosened the knot. "Do you want me to kiss you more? Touch you in a different way? Would you prefer I go slower? Go faster?"

"Not again," she managed to say. "We're not having sex again."

Something slammed through his gaze, something

fierce and determined. "Then we won't." He snatched her free of the sheet and swept her into his arms. "What happened in that bed… What's going to happen again, is something far more than sex."

"But it's not love." She groaned when his mouth closed over her throat, his teeth scraping the sensitive skin just beneath her ear. "This isn't The Inferno."

He tumbled to the bed with her. "There's no such thing as The Inferno," he insisted. Even as he spoke the words, he interlaced their hands until the heat erupted palm against palm. "And we've only known each other mere days. How could it be love?"

He slid over top of her, mating their bodies in one delicious stroke. She groaned, coherent thought fast becoming an impossibility. "Then what is this?" The words escaped in a choked gasp.

"I don't know. But I never want it to stop."

His movements escalated and he drove into her, hard and fast, racing toward that incredible peak he'd shown her earlier. How could the passion they shared be so strong and relentless, consuming them in great greedy gulps, and not last for all eternity? He didn't believe, and yet she felt the fire within him. He burned for her just as she burned for him, her body like dry tinder to his scorching touch.

They'd been together such a short time, and yet to be with him, surrounding him, inhaling him, inflamed for him, had become as vital to her as the air she breathed. Her feelings terrified her. They seemed to melt her down to her bare essence and reform her into something infinitely more.

Her climax caught her by surprise, slamming into

her and threatening to shatter her to the core. It ripped her apart, leaving her utterly exposed, every thought, every feeling there for him to see. And he must have seen, because he closed his eyes and covered her mouth with his, as though to keep the words unspoken.

And yet the kiss they shared said far more than any words could have expressed. The tenderness. The joy. The helpless want. The undeniable connection that existed between them. It was all there in that gentle benediction. Perhaps he sensed it, as well.

"We'll return home tomorrow," he told her again. "But we definitely won't be going our separate ways."

"So, how's married life treating you? You're celebrating your...what? Three-week anniversary?"

"To the day." Lazz flipped open the menu the waitress handed him and glanced across it at his brother. "And married life is fine."

"Fine," Sev repeated. "That's it...fine? Most men who've been married so short a time would describe it a bit differently. Incredible, maybe. Fantastic."

Lazz dropped the menu to the linen-draped tabletop. "My marriage to Ariana isn't real, as you damn well know." And wasn't that the biggest crock of manure he'd ever attempted to shovel.

"But you are still planning to keep that fact from Primo and Nonna, right?"

"Yes." Impatience edged Lazz's voice. "Penelope, too. Why the inquisition? What's going on?"

Sev turned to the waitress hovering at his elbow and placed his order, then waited while Lazz placed his, before answering. "No inquisition. I just wondered why you chose to have lunch with me instead of your beautiful wife."

"Ariana made plans with friends. In fact, she asked me which restaurant would afford the most privacy and best view, and I suggested Fruits de Mer. I expect she's around here someplace."

In fact, he knew it. He'd sensed his wife's presence the moment he'd walked in. The need to go in search of her had been nearly overwhelming, which was why he'd done just the opposite and taken a chair that kept his back to temptation. Not that he'd confess that small detail to his brother. It irritated Lazz enough that he had such a strong awareness of Ariana. He wasn't about to give Sev the opportunity to go off on one of his Inferno rants.

"You know, I brought Francesca to Fruits de Mer on our first official date." Humor drifted through Sev's eyes, turning them a burnished gold. "I think we lasted an entire five minutes before we went tearing over to my Pacific Heights place. We couldn't control ourselves."

"I assume you're going to blame that on The Inferno?"

"It was definitely a contributing factor." Sev's gaze dropped to Lazz's hands. "Wouldn't you agree?"

Lazz froze, suddenly aware that he was kneading his palm the same way his brothers and grandfather did. They'd always claimed it was one of the side effects of The Inferno, that when the connection formed during that first touch, it caused the bone-deep itch he'd been unable to suppress. Without a word, he picked up his glass of beer and took a long swallow.

To Lazz's relief, Sev changed the subject. "You didn't say who Ariana was lunching with."

"Maybe because I don't know. Friends." He shot his brother an inquiring glance. "Is she with Francesca?"

"Ariana isn't with any of the wives."

Lazz struggled to shove back a wave of irritation. "And you know this…how?"

"Because she's a half dozen tables behind you by the window. And her luncheon companion definitely isn't female."

Lazz stiffened and slowly turned. Ariana sat in a snug table for two close to a window perched above the Marina District. The sun plunged into the dense darkness of her hair, just as his hands had plunged into that silken mass during their time in Verdonia. She tilted her head in a way he'd seen countless times on their honeymoon, and the days since, and shards of ruby erupted from the ebony of her hair. From the back, her trim figure was showcased in a formfitting blaze of red that sculpted to her slender waist before cupping the curves of her hips and backside.

Oh, yeah. The woman was definitely Ariana. Which begged the question… Who the holy hell was the man with her?

The view from the window beside the two was one of the most incredible in the world, offering a stunning panorama of San Francisco Bay extending from the Golden Gate Bridge to Alcatraz. Not that either his wife or the man who so thoroughly held her attention noticed. Lazz caught the sound of her quick, husky laugh and watched as she reached out and squeezed the man's hand.

He heard a low, dangerous growl and didn't even realize he'd made the sound, any more than he remembered shooting to his feet. His hands collapsed into fists, and it took every ounce of self-control to keep them at his side. His focus narrowed, centering on his wife's back. Without a word to Sev, he stalked toward her table.

Seven

From: Lazzaro_Dante@DantesJewelry.com
Date: 2008, August 06 08:36 PDST
To: Bambolina@fornitore.it
Subject: Marriage Contract, Premarital Conditions...
Ad Nauseum

It occurs to me that I never asked whether you were romantically involved with someone else. In case you are...

Condition #5: We will both honor our vows for the duration of our marriage.

L.

From: Bambolina@fornitore.it
Date: 2008, August 06 17:45 CEST
To: Lazzaro_Dante@DantesJewelry.com

Subject: Re: Marriage Contract, Premarital Conditions…Ad Nauseam

Oh, Lazz. Allow me to ease your mind. I'm not currently involved with anyone. Are you?? Your fifth condition is not necessary. I would never cheat on my husband, even if he's a husband in name only. So no need to worry on that account or have an attack of the male jealousies.

Ciao! Ariana

From: Lazzaro_Dante@DantesJewelry.com
Date: 2008, August 06 08:49 PDST
To: Bambolina@fornitore.it
Subject: Re: Marriage Contract, Premarital Conditions…Ad Nauseum

No, I'm not involved with anyone, either. And FYI, I don't have male jealousies. It's not in my nature.

L.

"**I**'m serious, Ariana," the man said as Lazz approached. "You're going to have to make some changes or this won't work. I told you what I want, and you refuse to give it to me."

"You don't understand, Aaron. I can't. It's not who I am."

The man flicked a glance in Lazz's direction, the casual look changing to curiosity when Lazz paused beside their table. His wife glanced up at him, alarm blossoming in her widened eyes.

"Lazz? What are you doing here?"

He opened his mouth, planning to give his caveman impulses a voice. To his relief, he managed a more civilized response. "I'm having lunch with Sev." He kept his gaze fixed on her lunch companion as he addressed him. "Lazzaro Dante. I'm Ariana's husband."

The man climbed to his feet and offered his hand. "I'm Aaron Talbot. I'm—" Ariana gave a tiny shake of her head, and after a telling hesitation, he continued with barely a hitch. "I'm an old family friend. My father and Ariana's grandmother go way back."

If Sev hadn't chosen that moment to approach, Lazz didn't have any doubt that he'd have done or said something he'd have thoroughly enjoyed in the short term and eventually regretted given time. A lot of time.

"Hello, Ariana. Good to see you." Sev greeted his sister-in-law with a cool smile. He dropped a heavy hand on Lazz's shoulders. "Our lunch just arrived. You're coming, aren't you?"

Lazz resisted the pull for a full ten seconds. His attention switched to his wife. "Later," he promised.

Gathering up his self-control, he returned to their table. Sev motioned to the waitress, and a moment later she showed up with a tumbler containing two fingers of Jack Daniel's. She set it down in front of Sev, who shoved the glass across the table toward Lazz.

"Drink. Then tell me again that you don't believe in The Inferno."

"My reaction is perfectly logical," Lazz gritted out.

"And I'll testify to that at your murder trial." Sev speared a scallop. "Interesting."

Lazz closed his eyes. "I know I'm going to regret asking… What's interesting?"

"I didn't think The Inferno could only go in one direction. I guess I was wrong."

Lazz downed his drink in a single swallow, welcoming the burning heat as it shot straight to his stomach and poured through his veins. "I'm going to say this one last time. Ariana and I have not, nor will we ever, experience The Inferno. And there's an excellent reason for that."

"You're an idiot?"

The tumbler hit the table with a dull thud. "It doesn't exist. And what you've mistaken for jealousy is irritation that Ariana would conduct her…friendships—" and how the word scalded his tongue "—with such flagrant disregard. I'll suggest she be more discreet in the future so our marriage isn't exposed for the sham it's clearly become."

Sev leaned forward. "You might want to make that suggestion in a quieter voice than you're currently using and well outside of your wife's throwing range."

"This isn't a joke."

"No, marriage isn't. Nor is it a business proposition. I wish Dad had lived long enough to explain that fact to you. Since he didn't, I guess I'm stuck with the job."

Lazz frowned. Maybe he shouldn't have downed that whiskey quite so fast. "Now what are you talking about?"

"Haven't you ever wondered why Dad entered into that contract with Vittorio?"

Actually, he had. But with all the rush to slip the wedding in before Ariana turned twenty-five, he hadn't had time to pursue that aspect of the whole business. "The Romanos are broke, right? I assumed this was Dad's odd way of offering them a helping hand."

Skepticism swept across Sev's face. "A helping hand that's delayed for twenty years? A helping hand that's dependent on you and Ariana marrying?"

"No, you're right," Lazz said. "That doesn't make any sense."

"And why make Brimstone a part of the contract? Hell, why make a contract at all?" Sev pressed. "Just give Romano the damn stone."

Lazz shook his head. "I doubt Vittorio would have taken it. He may not have money, but he has more than his fair share of the Romano pride."

"And yet he sold his daughter to Dad. Why?"

Lazz winced at the harsh description. "I have no idea why he signed that contract. Ariana doesn't know, either. She said that Vittorio claimed it was Dad's idea, that he couldn't be talked out of it."

"Dad was so determined to have Vittorio sign that contract that he made Brimstone part of the deal. He was so determined to see you two married, that if you *didn't* marry, Brimstone would be disposed of. Why, Lazz?"

"How the hell should I know? Dad's gone."

"But Vittorio isn't. He must have some clue as to what Dad was thinking." Satisfied that he'd made his point, Sev leaned back in his seat. "I suggest you look into it."

Lazz studied his brother. He knew something— something he wasn't telling. "Why are you bringing this up now, after the fact? Why didn't you ask me to pursue it before Ariana and I married?" Understanding hit. "You know why Dad did it, don't you?"

"I have my suspicions. But since you're Mr. Facts and Figures, I'd rather you investigate this in your own meticulous fashion. Just be careful that when you add one and one together, that you don't come up with three."

"I'd rather you just told—"

Lazz caught a flash of red out of the corner of his eyes and turned. Ariana and Talbot had finished their lunch and were departing. As they wended their way through the tables, they spoke in low, furious voices, their heads close together. Not once did she look his way. Based on the intensity of her conversation, there wasn't a doubt in his mind that she'd forgotten all about him.

Time to remind her.

"Take care of the bill, will you?" Lazz shoved back his chair and stood. "And let them know at the office that I won't be in for the rest of the day."

Laughter glittered in Sev's eyes. "Last-minute change in plans?"

"A business meeting I forgot to attend," he corrected coolly. "A few contractual obligations I've neglected to address."

"Or undress?"

"Stuff it, Sev."

His wife and Talbot stood in the foyer where they exchanged a few final words. Then Talbot inclined his head and left the restaurant. Ariana stood there watching him, looking utterly devastated. Lazz came up behind her. Cupping her elbow, he ushered her outside into the brilliant early fall sunshine. Since they'd driven to the restaurant in Sev's car, he was without a vehicle, so he lifted an arm to summon a cab.

"What do you think you're doing?" she demanded in Italian.

A cab pulled up and Lazz opened the door. "I'm escorting my wife home."

"What if I don't want to go home?"

"I'd say that's too damn bad," he answered, switching to Italian.

He rattled off the address to the driver as he helped Ariana into the backseat. To his relief, she didn't fight him, possibly because she didn't want to cause a scene. Fumbling in her purse, she yanked out a pair of sunglasses and perched them on the end of her nose. Turning her head to look out the window, she didn't say another word until they reached an elegant apartment building.

They took the elevator to the penthouse, again in silence. Although the floor had originally housed two apartments, he'd taken them both over when he'd purchased the building and remodeled the space to better suit his needs. Unlocking the door, he stepped to one side. Ariana swept in ahead of him. Tossing her purse and sunglasses onto the foyer table, she swiveled to confront him.

"You are rude."

"And you, *wife,* are keeping secrets. Who is Talbot?"

She lifted a shoulder in a careless shrug. "Like he told you. He's an old family friend."

"So, if I pick up the phone and ask Vittorio or Constantine about Talbot, they'd describe him that way, too?" Her split-second hesitation gave her away. "I gather that would be a no."

"He's a family friend of Grandmother Penelope's. And yes, she would describe him just that way. Or rather, she'd describe his father that way."

His questions came rapid-fire. "You met the son through the father?"

"Yes."

"Is it serious between you?"

"We're not personally involved."

"Funny. You looked personally involved. In fact, you looked like you were having a lover's spat."

"Funny. That's what I thought *we* were doing." She turned on her heel with a graceful swing of her hips and crossed to the living room, affording him an exquisite view of a derriere lovingly outlined in red silk.

"This isn't a lover's spat," he replied, following her. "This is a termination discussion. As in, termination of our contract."

That caught her attention. She spun around to face him. "You wouldn't. The contract our parents signed requires that we remain together for three months. If you leave now, we lose the diamond. After all we've been through in order to preserve Brimstone, why would you throw it away at this late date?"

"Because I don't like being made a fool of. If you'd told me you had a lover—"

Angry color swept across her elegant cheekbones. "I don't. Haven't, as you know damn well."

"And is he the reason you didn't want to enter into a sexual relationship with me? I thought you understood that I don't like secrets." He approached, impressed by the way she continued to hold her ground. She lifted her chin, glaring through a sheen of tears that she was too proud to let fall. He felt the hum of tension gather strength, could feel the irresistible tug of it, demanding a surrender he refused to make. "Who is he, Ariana?"

This time she didn't bother with pretense. "I'm sorry, Lazz, but I can't tell you. I promised Penelope

I wouldn't discuss it long before you and I began our negotiations. But I assure you, he's not my lover."

"I want to believe you."

"But because of Marco and Caitlyn you find that difficult." It wasn't a question.

"Very difficult." He considered various options before reaching a decision. "I want your promise that you won't see him again."

She stared in dismay. "I…I don't think I can make that promise."

A wintry coldness settled over him. "Our marriage needs to remain intact for a little more than two months. If you want to resume your association with Talbot at that point, there's nothing I can or will say about it. But until then we have to act the part of newlyweds. That fiction isn't going to work if you're seen having intimate luncheons with another man."

"We were in public."

"You put your hands on him."

She stared blankly. "I did?"

"You put your hand over his and squeezed it."

"I—I don't remember." She closed her eyes and shook her head. "I'm sorry, Lazz. I'm a demonstrative person. I hug. I kiss. I touch people. It's who I am. Who I've always been."

"Not with Talbot. At least, not for the next nine weeks."

She looked at him then. He didn't want to notice how bone-white she'd gone. Or how her eyes grew black with pain. Clearly, Talbot meant something to her. Who would she have married, if not for that damnable contract? Who would have been her first lover?

The mere idea of Talbot putting his hands on Ariana shredded every ounce of Lazz's self-control.

He'd always prided himself on his ability to reason his way through any situation. Even with Caitlyn, after that one outburst in Marco's office, he'd been able to consider the situation from all angles and come to terms with it. He had a knack for compartmentalizing. He could logic his way through even the most emotional issues. He had an innate talent for tallying things up in tidy rows and columns. It took little-to-no effort to draw a line separating X from Y, a line that didn't allow any Zs to slip from one side to the other. But with Ariana...

He rubbed a hand along the back of his neck. Damn it to hell. Ariana sent his Zs all over the place.

"And if I refuse to stay away from Aaron?" she finally asked. "What will you do then?"

Aaron. Lazz's tidy columns melted right along with his temper. "Then I will personally take Brimstone and consign it to the deep blue. I won't be made a fool of by my wife. I won't allow the woman I married to sleep with another man while my ring is on her finger." He fought his way past a flood of emotions, unwanted emotions that ripped away every shred of civilized behavior. "I can't handle any more deception, Ariana. I won't tolerate any more secrets. This is the end."

Pain turned to temper, sparking a fire in Ariana's dark eyes. "Oh, please. You have as many secrets as I do. All people have them." The Italian lilt grew heavy in her voice. She approached—stalked—toward him, her anger growing with every step. "You made this 'no secrets' business a part of our marriage before we ever met. You demanded I confide in you before I had any idea what sort of man you are. How did I know I could trust you? Why should I open myself to such a risk?"

"Because those are the rules I play by."

"Rules? I'm talking about our marriage and you're spouting rules at me?" She flung her arms wide. "You expect me to walk into this contract marriage and strip myself bare for you. Have you done as much for me? I think not."

His own temper made a swift return, no matter how hard he attempted to tamp it down. "What secrets have I kept from you? I've answered every question you've asked, been as honest as I can."

"You kept The Inferno a secret." She cut off his incipient reply with a sweep of her hand. "And you lie to yourself, as well as to me, when you claim it doesn't exist. One touch from you and I'm ruined for any other man."

"Ruined?" He couldn't disguise how the word appealed to him. Apparently it didn't appeal to his wife quite as much.

Tears vied with temper. "Yes, ruined! But did you bother to warn me of that possibility? No!"

"The Inferno is the lie, not my denial of it."

"You think so?" She closed the distance between them and interlaced her fingers with his, sliding into the burn of palm against palm. Her hand tightened around his, deepening the connection. "Deny this, husband of mine. Deny your Dante heritage and whatever created this bond. Like it or not, we're stuck with each other."

The rush hit him, stronger than ever before. Like it? What a watered-down word to describe what he felt.

It wasn't just physical anymore. If that were the only connection between them, he wouldn't have been so furious when he'd discovered Ariana dining with another man. "It's lust." Truth became jumbled with self-preservation. "Desire."

Her fingers trembled within his. "You repeat those words like a mantra, when the truth is you're so determined to be logical that you can't see what's right in front of your nose. You are afraid of losing control. You are afraid that your heart will overrule your head. You are afraid to give yourself, fully, to another person."

"I'm not afraid," he denied. And he wasn't. He simply knew what he wanted in his life and, more importantly, what he didn't. "I'm pragmatic. Being pragmatic means I refuse to allow myself to be controlled by my emotions."

A hint of a smile curved a path across the lushness of her mouth. "So I noticed at lunch."

"I believe that proves my point," he bit back. "Don't you get it? I come from a passionate family, all of whom allow their emotions to overrule their common sense. And how has it benefited them?"

"The last time I looked, they all had strong, happy marriages."

"I'm sure my parents' marriage was the same when it first started out. But it doesn't last. And when it goes wrong, it goes very wrong. The minute you put your well-being in someone else's hands, you're going to get hurt."

Anger eased into compassion. "Life hurts, Lazz. You can't protect yourself from the bruises it doles out. Your relationship with Caitlyn is a perfect example of that. But you can allow someone else in, someone who's willing to share all of that with you. The pain. The joy. The sorrow. The laughter. Can't you open the door a crack? Allow nature to take its course and see where we end up in a few months."

"If we allow nature to take its course one more time, in a few months our twosome risks becoming a three-some," he said drily.

Soft color streaked across Ariana's cheekbones. "What's happened between us wasn't supposed to happen at all."

"It was inevitable," he said gently. "The only one who didn't know it was you."

"Lazz—"

"Shall I prove it to you?"

He didn't give her time to respond. He hooked his fingers around the lapels of her suit jacket and tugged. She didn't resist. Couldn't resist. It was beyond either of them. She came into his arms, fitting herself to him, a lock to a key. She'd asked him to let go of his control, to allow nature to take its course. He didn't have any other choice. Common sense vanished whenever he touched Ariana.

His hands eased into her hair, destroying the sophis-ticated little twist as he gave in to temptation. Her ir-resistible siren's call grew more powerful with each passing day. Did she even realize it emanated from her in the way she walked, in the way she looked at him, in every word she spoke? That despite what either of them claimed, their hunger for one another overrode every thought and intent?

He fell into the kiss. Fell into her warmth and the

generosity of her welcome. He never understood how she could open so utterly to him. And yet, she had from the very beginning. How did she allow herself such intense vulnerability when it was the one thing he most wanted to avoid? She gave so unstintingly that he couldn't just take. More than anything, he was driven to give back.

In that instant, the quality of their lovemaking changed. Slowed. Became more than a physical expression. One by one, he released the buttons of her suit jacket. It parted, revealing a scrap of black lace that cupped her breasts, the play of ebony against cream providing a visual feast.

"It's going to happen again, isn't it?" she asked.

"Without question."

A smile sweetened her expression, creating a fascinating dichotomy to her lush earthiness. She was a woman of endless facets and contradictions. An innocent sophisticate. A practical dreamer. An open mystery. And he wanted to know and explore each and every one of those facets.

He unclipped the front fastening of her bra and palmed the silken weight of her breasts. Her breath escaped in a low moan, and her head fell back. He swept his thumbs across the tips of her breasts, watching as desire caused them to flush and tighten. He couldn't remember the last time he'd seen anything that aroused him more. Lowering his head, he dragged his teeth across her nipple, then soothed it with his tongue.

Italian erupted from her, a strangled stream of plea and demand. He'd planned to keep the pace slow and leisurely. But she didn't give him that option. She tore at his shirt and tie, stripping them off him with impressive speed.

"Are we doing this here?" she demanded. "Now?"

He refused to make love to her again without proper protection. "No. We're doing this in my bedroom."

"Fine. The bedroom it is."

After kicking off her heels, she unzipped her narrow skirt and shimmied out of it. She straightened, standing before him in a black thong, garter belt and stockings. He must have groaned because laughter competed with the passion in her gaze. She threw herself against him and practically leaped into his arms. Her head nestled against his shoulder and waves of heavy, dark hair spilled across his arm in a silken curtain.

"Take me to your bedroom," she ordered. "Now."

He gathered her close. "If not sooner."

It was difficult enough to walk with the fullness of her breasts pressing against his chest. But her thighs—round, sleek thighs—wriggled within his grasp while her hip and the curve of her backside flirted with his groin. He had no idea how he made it the short distance from the living room to the bedroom without dumping them both on the floor and losing himself in her. Every step was sheer torture.

Lazz kicked the door closed behind him, enclosing them in dusky solitude. Muted sunshine filtered through the blinds, chasing after them as they reached the bed. He dropped Ariana to the mattress, not bothering to pull back the comforter. It was almost painful to strip off his trousers and shorts. At the last minute he remembered protection.

He yanked open the bedside drawer, pulling it free

of its mooring and dumping it onto the floor. He swore in frustration and then swore again when Ariana slipped off the bed. "Wait," he said. "Let me—"

"I've got it."

She gathered up one of the foil squares and fumbled slightly with the wrapper, betraying her inexperience and rousing a fierce wave of tenderness in him. Then she ripped it open and removed the circle of latex. There was a hint of curiosity in her expression as she examined it, before turning her attention to him.

She shook her head in dismay. "This will never fit. Have you nothing larger?"

If his need hadn't been so dire, he'd have laughed. "It fits," he said. "Give it to me. I'll do it."

"No, no. Let me." She fit the latex over him and cautiously rolled it down his length. She caught her lip between her teeth. "Am I hurting you?"

"You're killing me."

She froze. "Should I stop?"

"No. Not unless you want to drive me straight out of my mind."

A tiny laugh slipped free. She struggled to contain it, without success. "I'm not laughing at you, I promise. It's…" She waved a hand as though to summon the right words. "Look at us. We have no clothes. All we want is to make love. We are desperate."

"Very desperate."

"If we don't make love right this instant, you have assured me we will either expire or go insane."

"Any second now it'll be over," he confirmed.

"And I haven't a clue what I'm doing."

He grinned. "You're making me laugh at a totally inappropriate time. That's never happened to me before."

"Me, neither." His gorgeous, sophisticated wife grinned like a street urchin. "It is funny, yes?"

"Oh, yeah."

"Give me a minute and I'll be serious again."

"I don't want you serious." And he didn't. "Just be yourself."

For some reason that caused her laughter to fade. He'd already bared her, physically. Now he watched as she bared her emotions, betraying the gentle want, the soft hunger. The need for him, and him alone.

Slowly, her hands moved again, stroking him into hardness. When she was done, she bent slightly to remove her garter and stockings, and her hair swirled forward across her shoulders. The sheer grace and sensuality of her impacted like a blow. Unable to help himself he caressed the vulnerable spot at the nape of her neck and followed the pure silken line from there down to the base of her spine.

She shuddered beneath his touch and whispered something in Italian. Whether plea or confession, he didn't quite catch it. But when she straightened, the last of her clothing formed a dark pool at their feet. Together they fell back onto the comforter, and he mated their bodies.

They moved slowly at first, taking those first few moments to reacquaint themselves with the fit and feel and flow of one into the other. "Oh, yes. Like that," she murmured.

He gave to her. And then he gave more, taking the

time to unlock the subtle secrets of her body, the movements and caresses that were unique to her and caused her to soar to places she'd never been before. The burn came. The flame that connected them exploded with heat and light and pleasure as it consumed them.

Lazz felt her quiver beneath him, teetering for an endless second on that pinnacle between climb and tumble. Her breath caught, held, and then burst from her lungs as she shot up and over into a helpless free fall. He didn't hesitate. He leapt with her.

And he lost himself in her. In this woman. In his wife. Within that intense release came a shattering, and all he could do was surrender to it.

Eight

From: Bambolina@fornitore.it
Date: 2008, August 07 11:22 CEST
To: Lazzaro_Dante@DantesJewelry.com
Subject: Marriage Contract, Premarital Conditions…
me again!
I just thought of one more thing. I hope you don't
mind. And I hope your apartment is big enough!
Counter-Condition #3: I require a room for my
private use, one that you promise not to enter.
Ciao! Ariana

From: Lazzaro_Dante@DantesJewelry.com
Date: 2008, August 07 09:04 PDST
To: Bambolina@fornitore.it
Subject: Re: Marriage Contract, Premarital Condi-
tions…me again!

What the hell is this about? I'm serious. What do you need a private room for? I'm going to call. We need to discuss this.

L.

Ariana regarded her grandmother with a hint of exasperation. "I can't believe I agreed to this."

"And I can't thank you enough, especially considering you're still practically on your honeymoon." Penelope said.

"One month tomorrow," Ariana confirmed before shaking her head. "What in the world made you suggest I attend this benefit in your place? Mrs. Pennywinkle has never made a public appearance before. Nor has she ever had a representative."

"They caught me at a weak moment," Penelope confessed. "It's for children who are burn victims. Once they promised no media attendance, how could I refuse?"

Ariana softened. "You couldn't, of course. Are you certain you don't want to go yourself?"

One look at her grandmother's face answered that question. "I can't run the risk I'll have a panic attack and frighten the children."

"Never mind," Ariana soothed. "I'm happy to stand in for you."

"Thank you. I was hoping you'd say that." A hint of mischief glittered in Penelope's eyes. "I also had an ulterior motive for my request."

"You thought it would convince me to do everything in my power to become the new Mrs. Pennywinkle?"

"I can't fool you, can I? I even had your Nancy doll flown in for the occasion. I thought it would make a nice prop. You have no idea how much I've longed to attend a charity event—" Penelope broke off with a sigh.

"Don't." Ariana stooped beside Penelope and enfolded her in a tight embrace. "You've done so much for the family. Worked so hard. I just wish you'd let me explain to Lazz. It's been weeks since he saw me with Aaron. Even though he doesn't mention it, it's still there between us."

Penelope shook her head, adamant. "The Dantes are under constant media scrutiny. I know they'd agree to keep my secret." She gazed intently at her granddaughter. "But secrets have a way of getting out."

Ariana flinched. She sincerely hoped not. At least, she hoped certain secrets didn't get out. "He's my husband, Gran," she insisted gently. "He has a right to know."

"Maybe once Aaron Talbot agrees to take you on as the new Mrs. Pennywinkle, we could reconsider."

"*If* Aaron agrees," Ariana corrected. "After our luncheon meeting, I'd have to say it's going to be difficult to convince him. He's determined to keep Mrs. Pennywinkle sacrosanct."

Penelope dismissed that with a wave of her hand. "He'll give in. He won't have any choice if he wants more Mrs. Pennywinkle books. And once you're the new Mrs. P, the media attention will be on you. They might have a passing interest in me, but once I'm back with Carolina and Vittorio on the Romano estate, they won't have the opportunity to approach me unless I choose to let them." Pain and fear added definition to her wrinkles. "It won't be like it was after the accident."

"No, it won't." Ariana kissed her grandmother's cheek and straightened. "I'd better go or I'll be late."

"Will you come back to the hotel room afterward and tell me how it went?" Penelope asked.

Ariana shook her head. "I'll have to fill you in tomorrow. I'm supposed to meet Lazz for dinner, and that won't give me much time to get back to the apartment before he returns from work."

"Be careful with your doll. I'd be crushed if it were lost or damaged. She's the very first one ever made."

Ariana smiled indulgently. "I remember. I wouldn't dream of allowing any harm to come to her."

Penelope nodded in relief. "Try and have fun."

That would be a stretch. Still, she would do everything in her power to make it a special occasion for the children. Giving her grandmother a final hug and kiss, Ariana picked up the Nancy doll Penelope had given her as a child and left the hotel room.

"Are we all set?" Lazz asked one of the benefit organizers. "I'm hoping this Pennywinkle representative will be an acceptable substitute for the author. Fortunately, the publisher sent free autographed copies of Pennywinkle's book, so that should please the children."

He also hoped the representative didn't have an adverse reaction to some of the more severely deformed burn victims. Of all the Dantes, he was the most passionate about this particular organization and worked tirelessly on its behalf. He'd hate to think what should have been a special treat for the children might turn into a nightmare of rejection.

"I believe the rep just arrived," the organizer replied, nodding toward the ballroom doorway.

Lazz turned to look, then grinned. "That's not Pennywinkle's rep. That's my wife."

"Oh, of course," the man hastened to say. "I guess it was the Nancy doll that fooled me."

Lazz took a second look. Ariana stood near the doorway, shaking hands with the assistant he'd assigned as the "official greeter" for Mrs. Pennywinkle's representative. And in her arms she cuddled a Nancy doll. After excusing himself, he left the small group of organizers to their last-minute details and joined his wife.

"Fancy meeting you here," he greeted her.

For some reason she didn't look thrilled to see him. Shocked might be a more appropriate description. "Lazz? What are you doing here?"

"I sit on the board of the organization. I'm the one responsible for today's benefit." He cocked his head to one side. "And you?"

She hesitated for a telling moment. "Mrs. Pennywinkle is an old family friend. She asked if I'd represent her."

Interesting. There wasn't time to ask further questions, but he had to admit he was curious to know more about the reclusive author. "I'm glad you're here," he said simply. "Let me introduce you to the children."

She linked her fingers with his, and the distinctive tug hit the instant their palms joined, a ribbon of desire that continued to connect them even as the program began. Over the next hour, lunch was served. While everyone ate, Ariana read from the latest Mrs. Pennywinkle book and cuddled one of the children on her lap. Lazz held the book and turned the pages for her.

He wondered if she realized her emotional reactions to the situation caused a hint of an Italian lilt to weave its way through her voice. If anyone else picked up on it, they didn't let on. But he noticed. He noticed something else, as well. He noticed how his wife maneuvered from table to table, never seeming to rush. Never seeming too busy to speak to or hug or laugh with each and every child.

Toward the end of the event, she joined the very last table and sat with one of the more severely burned children, a painfully shy little girl. Although the child carried a tattered Mrs. Pennywinkle book, she was the only one so far who didn't also have a Nancy doll clutched in her arms.

"Does Cecelia not like dolls?" Ariana whispered to the mother at one point.

Bright color swept across the woman's cheekbones as she shook her head. "We can't afford one," she replied stiffly. "Maybe for Christmas."

Lazz watched as tears gathered in his wife's eyes. Turning to the little girl, Ariana indicated the doll she'd brought with her to the event. "Did you know this is the first Nancy doll ever made?"

Cecelia stared, wide-eyed. "The very first?" She reached toward the doll's ruffled skirt before jerking her hand back. "I'm sorry," she whispered.

"You can touch her. In fact…" Ariana settled the doll carefully in Cecelia's arms. "This Nancy doll is magical, maybe because she was the first. Her job is to live her life the same way she does in the storybooks. She wants to be with someone she can help. Otherwise her magic will fade away."

Cecelia froze, hardly daring to breathe. "She wants to be with someone like me?"

"Just like you," Ariana confirmed. "She's to stay with you until you don't need her any longer."

Cecelia bit down on her lip. "What if that's a long, long time? What if the operations take years and years?"

It took Ariana a moment to reply. "Nancy will stay with you for as long as necessary. And when you don't need her any longer, then it's your job to pass her on to someone else who does."

The little girl stared up at Ariana, a mixture of adoration and determination reflected in her ruined face. "I will," she promised fervently. "I'll give her to someone who needs her as bad as me."

Lazz could only imagine how difficult it must have been for his wife to give away her treasured doll. But when it was done, she stood, smiled at everyone and then walked away without once looking back. After excusing himself, he went after her and took her arm. She didn't require his physical support, but there wasn't a question in his mind that she desperately needed him emotionally.

"Hang on just a minute. It's almost over."

He stopped at the dais long enough to give a brief speech thanking everyone for attending and wrapping up the event. He didn't have a moment's doubt that the children would remember this occasion for years to come. Finally, he gestured toward the side door.

"Let's go."

"I can manage," she insisted.

He could hear the strain dragging through each

word. He didn't reply. He simply ushered her into the hallway. The minute the door closed behind them, he wrapped her up in a tight embrace and kissed her. She stiffened within his hold, resisting him for all of five seconds before dissolving, responding to him as passionately as every other time he touched her.

Eventually he pulled back and regarded her with a tender expression.

"Are you all right? I imagine giving that doll away was one of the most difficult things you've ever done."

She didn't deny it. "Helping others, paying it forward. It's what Mrs. Pennywinkle stands for. It's the message that underscores every single one of her books. How could I not honor the true meaning of the Nancy doll by passing her along the same way all the children do between the pages of the Pennywinkle books?"

"You couldn't. It's not in your nature." He draped a comforting arm around her shoulders. "Come on. What do you say we go home?"

"Sounds perfect."

When they reached the apartment, Ariana took Lazz's hand in hers. Instead of leading him to the nearest bed, she paused by the door to the room she'd requested for her third marital condition. She opened it without a word and flipped on the lights.

He walked in and stared, stunned. "My God." He took his time, moving through the room, examining painting after painting. "You did these, didn't you? I'd recognize your artwork anywhere."

"Yes, they're mine. Most of them I painted while in Italy. They're for a new Pennywinkle book. At least, they might be, depending on what Aaron decides." She took a deep breath and faced him. "Aaron Talbot publishes the Mrs. Pennywinkle series. That's why we were meeting at lunch the other day. He's considering me as a replacement for the previous Mrs. Pennywinkle."

"It was a business meeting?" Lazz winced. That finally answered his question about Talbot, and he couldn't begin to express the relief he felt, as well as his remorse over his earlier suspicions. "I'm so sorry, Ariana. I really am an ass, aren't I?"

"Occasionally." She smiled to soften her response. "And your apology is accepted. Sometimes it's hard to reach an accurate conclusion when you don't have all the facts."

"Sev warned me of that. But that still doesn't excuse my reaction." Lazz studied the paintings and shook his head. "These are amazing. I assume Talbot has agreed to take you on?"

"Not yet."

That caught him by surprise. "He hasn't already snapped you up as the new Pennywinkle? Is he crazy?"

Ariana laughed, though he heard a hint of anguish underscoring her amusement. "I happen to think so. So does Gran."

Just like that, it clicked. "Penelope. Penny. Pennywinkle. *She's* Mrs. Pennywinkle."

Ariana nodded. "She started painting as a form of therapy after her car accident. Now that her arthritis makes it too difficult to continue, she wants me to take over."

"I don't understand." He glanced over his shoulder

at her. "If Penelope's the real Pennywinkle, why didn't she attend the benefit?"

"One of the side effects of being trapped for two days in a wrecked car is that she suffers from panic attacks. The intense media attention afterward only made her more fearful. She refuses to make appearances in case she has an attack and frightens the children."

Compassion swept through him. "Losing control like that would be difficult for anyone, but it must be especially tough for a woman of her strength of character."

"Extremely."

Lazz returned his attention to his wife's artwork. He'd been impressed when he'd seen the sketches she'd done while on their honeymoon. He'd even gone out of his way to rescue and salvage her sketch pad because he couldn't bear the thought of losing such amazing drawings. But those were mere shadows of what she'd accomplished here.

"You've actually shown these to Talbot? And he rejected them?"

"Not exactly. I showed him a portfolio of my work. He rejected that. He says my illustrations are too whimsical. And those are nowhere near as whimsical as these. What he really wants is for me to copy my grandmother's style so no one knows there's been a change in authorship. I tried to do what he asked." She crossed to a stack of canvasses leaning against the wall and removed one of them, pulling back the cloth covering. "This is how they come out."

"Ouch."

"My reaction, exactly."

"There are other publishers, Ariana, any number of whom would be delighted to produce a new, updated Mrs. Pennywinkle. Have you considered approaching someone else?"

"According to Aaron, our contract prohibits it."

"Why don't you give me a copy of the contract, and I'll have my lawyers take a look? If they don't see an out, we'll hire a literary attorney."

"I'm not sure my grandmother will agree. She has a long history with Aaron's father. But I'll ask her." Ariana gave Lazz a quick kiss, just a swift brush of her lips against his. "Thank you."

That one fleeting caress was all it took. If he lived to be a hundred, he didn't think he'd ever understand exactly what it was about Ariana that moved him so. That took him from down-to-earth common sense and shot him straight into molten need.

He didn't say a word. He didn't have to. He heard the slight hitch in her breathing, saw comprehension darken her eyes to ebony. A light flush gave definition to her cheekbones. And the air around them thickened, grew heavy and scented with the perfume of their want.

Without taking his eyes off her, he tugged at the knot in his tie and yanked it free. Ariana followed suit, stripping out of the clothes she'd changed into after their return to the apartment. And yet, still they didn't touch, not until the last bit of silk and cotton carpeted the floor.

Then they came together. Slowly. Gently. Softly. There in a room that contained his wife's soul, he joined with her. Gave to her. Gifted her with all he had within him. Just as she had sacrificed her doll, he sacrificed his disbelief. He gave himself up to her, gave himself up to The Inferno.

He gave himself up to love.

Ariana moaned. "I don't think I can move."

"Join the club."

"I'm also starving," she confessed. "Why don't we order in? That way we don't have to move any farther than the phone."

"Dinner? Is it that late?" He checked his watch and swore. "You're going to have to move a lot farther than that. And faster, too. Your father is due over any minute."

She bolted upright, panic shooting through her. The past month had been sheer agony while she'd waited for either the phone call from her father informing her that he'd found Brimstone and saved her from guaranteed damnation or for her world to come crashing down when Lazz discovered how she'd deceived him. It would appear the wait was over.

She burst into nervous Italian. "Papa? Here? Why is he coming here? I thought he was back home."

"I asked him to bring Brimstone over."

She went absolutely rigid. "Now? But... Aren't we supposed to split Brimstone on our three-month anniversary? What's the rush?"

Lazz shot her a curious look. "In order to determine the diamond's value, I need to have it appraised. That doesn't happen overnight. I asked Vittorio to bring the diamond to San Francisco sometime this week."

"And Papa agreed? He brought it?" she asked tautly.

"He flew in today."

She relaxed slightly and drew a slow, calming breath. "I wonder why he didn't let me know. That's good news." She grinned, reveling in the joyful relief that washed over her. "Actually, that's great news."

He scooped her close. "And we're not splitting the stone, remember? The Dantes are buying you out. Very bad luck to split Brimstone."

"Really?" she asked, intrigued. "Why is that?"

"According to legend, the only way Brimstone can be split is if—"

She lifted an eyebrow. "Hell freezes over?"

He grinned at the play on words. "Close enough. No, according to legend, Brimstone has to split on its own. And diamonds don't normally do that. Not without a bit of help.

"So, until that happens, your family plans to keep it intact?" At his nod, she asked, "What do you get when it splits on its own? You do get something, right?"

"Rich."

She smothered a laugh. "That's what the legend says?"

"No, that's what I say. The legend says we'll receive good fortune and God's favor until the Dante line is no more. The Dantes are big on superstition, if not reality. Everything from The Inferno to Brimstone."

Before she could argue the point, the doorbell sounded and they both jumped to their feet, yanking on clothes with careless haste. Lazz finished dressing first. "Take your time," he told Ariana. "I'll delay your father."

She joined them just as Vittorio greeted Lazz with a handshake that didn't quite hide his nervousness. "I hope you don't mind that I'm a few minutes early."

"Not at all." Lazz gestured toward the wet bar. "Can I get you something to drink?"

"Scotch and water," Vittorio requested. "A double."

The request had Ariana's heart stuttering. She tried to catch his eye, but he refused to look at her. And that's when she knew. He hadn't found the diamond, and he'd come here to confess his sins. She shut her eyes. Please, no. Please let her be mistaken. Please don't let her marriage end before it had fully begun.

Lazz fixed the drink and offered it to Vittorio. "What's wrong?" he asked quietly.

"I was hoping to delay this conversation for a while longer. But clearly, I cannot."

"I assume that means that you don't have Brimstone," Lazz said without inflection. "Is that what you're here to tell me?"

"Yes." Vittorio downed his drink in a single swallow. "That's what I'm here to tell you."

Ariana closed her eyes. "Oh, Papa," she murmured.

"I tried to call and warn you, *bambolina,* but—"

Lazz cut in, fighting to keep his voice level. "What happened to the diamond? Where is it?"

Vittorio hesitated. "After Dominic's death, I removed the stone from the safety deposit box where we'd agreed to keep it," he confessed.

Ariana dropped into the nearest chair. "After Dominic died?" she repeated in disbelief. No. No, that wasn't what he'd told her before the wedding. He'd said… She struggled to recall. He'd *implied* that he'd only recently lost it. "It's been gone all these years?"

"I'm afraid so." Vittorio cleared his throat. "Primo had no idea Dominic had taken the diamond in the first place, so after his death I wanted to return it and explain how it came to be in my possession."

"Of course," Lazz said evenly. "It was the only option available to you since disposing of the diamond in any other manner would have been unethical."

Vittorio had the grace to redden. "This was my feeling, as well," he was quick to assure. "But before I could return it, it went missing. I searched everywhere for it. It was as though it had vanished into thin air. I can only assume one of the servants…" He trailed off with a lifted shoulder.

"And you've spent the last dozen or more years searching for it? I assume you called in the authorities?" Lazz lifted an eyebrow. "No?"

"No," Vittorio admitted. "I didn't say anything when I lost Brimstone because I was too ashamed to admit to my carelessness. On top of that there would have been a scandal." He spared Lazz an apprehensive glance. "But there's another reason. A more important reason I allowed the wedding to go through."

Ariana crossed to his side and took her father's hand in hers. "What, Papa?"

He caressed his daughter's cheek. "Dominic wanted this marriage with all his heart. He insisted on the contract, even over my express objections." He addressed Lazz again. "He did it to protect you, my boy. And he made Brimstone part of the deal because he knew it was the only way to convince me to go along with his crazy scheme. Now that he's gone—" Vittorio broke off and gathered himself before continuing. "I wish to honor his wishes."

"I'm sure your reasons for insisting Ariana and I go

through with the marriage were totally altruistic." Lazz made the comment in a wintry voice.

"It was because of The Inferno," Vittorio continued doggedly. "Out of respect for your privacy I haven't wanted to mention something so personal, but your father saw a spark between you and my daughter all those years ago. That's why he insisted on the contract."

"Enough," Lazz snapped.

Ariana gazed at him, stricken. "Lazz, please," she whispered.

He glared at Vittorio. "I can make a fairly logical guess why you didn't tell my family you lost Brimstone. You were hoping that despicable contract never came to light. After all, my father was dead, and supposedly none of the other Dantes knew about it, any more than they knew what happened to Brimstone. Its whereabouts died with my father."

"No, I—"

Lazz cut him off. "Of course, if the agreement did turn up, you hoped it wouldn't happen until after Ariana's twenty-fifth birthday so that you could claim the diamond had been disposed of as per the terms of the contract. But when Caitlyn unexpectedly came across Dad's copy of the agreement in a box of old family papers and brought it to my attention *before* Ariana turned twenty-five, it didn't leave you any choice."

"You seem to have all the answers," Vittorio said with a dispirited shrug. "Feel free to finish it."

"Very well." Lazz addressed his remarks to Ariana. "Your father had two options. He could either admit the truth and deal with the suspicion and fury of the Dantes.

And I guarantee, not only would Primo have been livid over that contract, he'd have also been highly skeptical about the diamond's convenient disappearance, especially considering the Romanos' precarious financial situation. Or your father had a second option. He could pretend that Brimstone was still safe and sound. He could allow the marriage to go through and...hope. Hope that our marriage worked out and all would be forgiven. Hope that the Dantes wouldn't want to cause a scandal involving the Romanos, especially now that the two families were connected by marriage. Hope that a miracle would happen and Brimstone would be found."

"Actually, you're wrong about that last part," Ariana corrected. "My father didn't hope any such thing."

Lazz shot a sharp look at his wife, and she could see suspicion take hold, one he visibly fought to suppress. "I was wrong about Aaron, so I don't want to make that same mistake again," he told her. "But how do you know what your father thought or didn't think?"

She lifted her chin and looked straight at him. "Because *he* didn't take those possibilities into consideration before we married. *I* did. I married you to protect my family from the Dantes."

Nine

From: Lazzaro_Dante@DantesJewelry.com
Date: 2008, August 07 10:57 PDST
To: Bambolina@fornitore.it
Subject: Marriage Contract, Premarital Conditions…
Final

As per our phone conversation, I'm sending you my final premarital condition.

Condition #6: Dantes will have Brimstone appraised by two (2) independent sources. Dantes will retain possession of Brimstone. The Romanos will receive a cash settlement of one half the appraised value of the diamond.

I hope this meets with your approval. Looking forward to the 28th.

L.

From: Bambolina@fornitore.it
Date: 2008, August 07 20:20 CEST
To: Lazzaro_Dante@DantesJewelry.com
Subject: Re: Marriage Contract, Premarital Conditions...Final

Oh, Lazz. You make me laugh. I, too, am looking forward to the 28th. However you decide to divide Brimstone is fine with me and my family.
Ciao! Ariana

Ariana's confession hung in the air for an endless minute.

Then Lazz turned to her father. "Please excuse us," he said with biting formality. "Your daughter and I need to speak in private."

Alarm flared in Vittorio's dark eyes. "I won't leave her alone with you. Not while you're so furious."

"He won't hurt me," Ariana reassured. "And he's right, Papa. This is between the two of us."

Lazz didn't wait for an argument to erupt. He simply opened the front door and stood there. Without another word, Vittorio left. Hanging on to his self-control through sheer willpower, Lazz gently closed the door. "Just to clarify, you knew before we married that Brimstone was missing?" he asked.

Ariana nodded. "My father told me right before the ceremony." She retreated behind a facade of calm poise. If the circumstances had been different, it would have impressed the hell out of him. "He neglected to mention how long the diamond had been missing, or I might have made a different decision."

"So, you've been lying to me from the start."

She didn't spare herself. "Yes. At the time I found out about Brimstone, I didn't know you other than through a few terse e-mails and a stilted phone conversation or two. What little I did know warned that you wouldn't react well to the news. So I did what I felt I had to."

"You were right," he said. Her head jerked up at that. "I'm not reacting well to the news."

She was foolish enough to cross the room toward him. "Try and see this from my point of view, Lazz. I hoped my father would find the diamond before anyone discovered it was missing. What I didn't count on was The Inferno." Her thumb traced a shaky path across her palm as she confessed with devastating honesty. "I also didn't count on falling in love with you."

"Don't," he bit out. He took a step back, putting some distance between them and the relentless pull that even now urged him to surrender to his feelings for Ariana. The connection should have broken. It should have shattered when she confessed what she'd done. But it hadn't. If anything, the more he resisted, the more unrelenting it grew. "You expect me to believe you love me when everything about our relationship has been a lie? Every condition of our marriage a joke?"

Her chin shot up. "The only thing I lied about was Brimstone," she insisted. "The rest was real."

"It's all been a lie. Mrs. Pennywinkle. Brimstone." He fixed a wintry gaze on her. "The Inferno."

Anger flared, turning her eyes to jet. "Fine. I didn't tell you about Mrs. Pennywinkle and Brimstone. I was protecting my family, and I refuse to apologize for that, especially considering that in my position, you'd have done the same thing. But the rest…" She held out her hand, palm up. "The rest of it is real. My feelings for you are real. The Inferno is real."

Ice encased him. "I was betrayed before. You knew that. And yet, you still chose to betray me again. I won't stay with a woman I can't trust."

She turned deathly pale. "We can work through this. Please, Lazz, won't you try?"

He wavered for a brief moment. Only hours earlier, for a brief, shining moment, he'd believed. The Inferno had lived in him, even if it had been an illusion. He wanted the dream again, was desperate for another taste of the fantasy, regardless of the personal cost.

He forced himself to take another step back before he lost all he held most dear. Reason. Common sense. Clear-cut lines and tidy columns. "We married for business," he informed her. "That business has now been concluded."

Her arm dropped to her side, and her fingers curled inward on her palm, like a flower blossom closing against the chill night air. "There's no longer any reason for our marriage to continue, is there?" She asked the question in Italian.

"No logical reason."

He flinched as he witnessed the death of hope. She lifted her chin, hanging on to her dignity by a shred. "I realize this is your apartment, but if you'd give me an hour or two of privacy, I'll remove my things."

"Ariana—"

"Please, Lazz."

Her voice broke apart on his name, a shattering that

went from voice to heart to spirit. He started to say something, then changed his mind. There was nothing left to be said. Without another word, he turned on his heel and walked out.

Ariana stood in the middle of Lazz's apartment less than an hour later and stared at her grandmother. All around her were the bits and pieces of the life she'd shared with Lazz, like flotsam adrift after a shipwreck. "I'm really happy to see you, Gran, so don't misunderstand my question," she said. She fought a wave of exhaustion that threatened to knock her off her feet. "But why are you here?"

"Lazz called. He said I should come over immediately. He's filled me in on most of what's happened."

"He called you?" Ariana couldn't hold back her tears. Considering how they'd parted, it was an incredibly kind gesture on his part. "Why would he do that?"

"I assume he's worried about you. It's an excellent quality to have in a husband." She wheeled herself farther into the living room. "Since I'd already arranged for my driver to transport me over here, it worked out well for all concerned."

"You were coming for a visit?" Ariana asked. Unannounced? That wasn't like Penelope. She wouldn't intrude without calling first. "You're welcome, of course. I just don't understand why…"

"I have two items to discuss with you. I was going to postpone them both until I heard your father had flown in to see Lazz. There could only be one reason. He was finally going to admit the truth about Brimstone. As soon as I heard that, I rushed over." She gave her wheelchair a disgruntled smack. "Not that either of us can actually rush anymore."

Ariana froze, zeroing in on the most critical of her grandmother's comments. "You know about Brimstone?"

"I do." Fire flashed in her grandmother's blue eyes. "I know about both Brimstone and that despicable contract. I've known for years. How your father could do something so unconscionable I'll never understand."

"He says—"

Penelope cut her off. "I know what excuses he's given. All that nonsense about The Inferno."

Ariana closed her eyes. "It's not nonsense," she said softly.

"No?" A hint of humor mitigated her grandmother's fury. "I was hoping you'd say that. It must be the romantic in me. Not that it matters. If what you and Lazz felt as children really was a form of The Inferno, then Vittorio and Dominic should have waited and let nature take its course. Your parents should have separated you two until you were old enough to meet as fully grown adults. At that point, you could have formed an attachment—or not—without involving contracts and diamonds and temporary marriages. Instead they decided to give new depth and definition to the word 'idiotic' and mucked up the entire affair."

"It's too late to change anything now, Gran. What's done is done."

Penelope lifted an eyebrow. "So nature hasn't taken its course?" she asked delicately.

Ariana bit back a tear-laden laugh. "Oh, it's taken

its course. But because Papa lost the diamond and I knew it before we married, Lazz doesn't trust me anymore. With some justification, I have to admit."

"Hmm." Penelope's mouth compressed in annoyance. "I suspect I've contributed to that problem, as well. Or at least Mrs. Pennywinkle has."

Ariana sank into a chair next to her grandmother and joined hands with her. "There were a lot of contributing factors. Secrets on top of secrets. Aaron and Mrs. Pennywinkle. Papa and Dominic. Brimstone. Now that the diamond's gone, it gives him the excuse he needs to pull away before he gets burned."

Penelope patted Ariana's hand. "Yes, well. That can be dealt with in time. But first things first. Brimstone isn't gone. I have it." She gave a little shrug. "Well, technically, you have it."

Ariana stared in shock. "I have it? Where?"

"In your Nancy doll. When your father removed the diamond from the safe deposit box and brought it home, it gave me the opportunity to put paid to that disgraceful contract once and for all. I took the diamond and sewed it inside the doll. I decided that if there was no diamond, there wouldn't be a marriage." She sniffed. "Little did I know your father would prove more determined than I anticipated."

Ariana struggled to draw breath. "Wait, wait. Go back." Please, please let there have been a mistake. "You put Brimstone in my Nancy doll? The one you had flown out here for the charity event? *That* Nancy doll?"

"Of course *that* Nancy doll. What other one is there? To be honest, I had it couriered out here because I knew that at some point Vittorio would be forced to produce the diamond. When he couldn't, he'd have to admit what he'd done." Her smile would have done a canary-swallowing cat proud. "I've been looking forward to that moment for years. I'm just sorry I missed it."

"Why would you allow me to take that doll to the charity function, knowing it contained a diamond worth millions?" Ariana could barely articulate the question. "Why would you allow me to take such a risk?"

Penelope stirred uneasily. "You'd never let anything happen to that doll. It means more to you than anything you've ever owned. If the entire villa were aflame, Nancy would be the one possession you'd grab on your way out the door." Something in Ariana's expression must have given her away. Penelope turned chalk-white. "You do still have the doll, don't you?

Ariana shook her head. "No." The word was barely more than a whisper. "I gave her away. I gave Nancy away."

"What do you mean? What are you talking about?"

"There was a little girl at the charity event. A burn victim. She was the only child without a doll. So…so I gave her mine and told her to pass the doll along when she didn't need it any longer."

"Oh, Ariana, how could you do such a thing?"

Ariana stiffened. "I don't care how many diamonds are hidden in that doll," she snapped. "It was the right thing to do. If you'd met Cecelia, you'd have done the same."

Penelope held up her hands. "You're right. Of course, you're right. Maybe I'd have removed the diamond first, but nevertheless." She waved that aside. "That still doesn't solve our problem. What are we going to do?"

Ariana folded her arms across her chest. "Absolutely nothing. I refuse to take the doll away from that child or attempt to substitute it with another. If Lazz or one of the Dantes wants to approach her, that's on them. But as far as I'm concerned, it was fate. That diamond should have been thrown in the ocean long ago, right along with that hideous contract." Not to mention every last one of the conditions she and Lazz had negotiated.

"I can't say I disagree. Even so…" Penelope frowned. "Is your marriage really over, dearest? Can nothing be done to salvage it?"

Ariana's bravado faded. "With Brimstone gone, so is my reason for marrying Lazz. The only excuse I have for remaining in San Francisco is if Aaron wants me to write and illustrate the Mrs. Pennywinkle books. Maybe if that happens, Lazz and I will have time—" The expression on Penelope's face had Ariana closing her eyes in distress. "You told me there were two reasons you were on your way over here. One was Brimstone. I assume the other was to tell me you heard from Aaron."

"He's rejected you as my replacement. I'm so sorry."

"Lazz planned to have some lawyers look over your contract." Ariana gave a humorless laugh. "I don't think that's likely to happen anytime soon. Do you?"

Her grandmother shook her head. "No, I guess not. So, what now?"

Ariana looked around the apartment in silent fare-well. "The only logical alternative available. I'll return to Italy." Penelope started to say something then hesitated. An odd expression drifted across her face, one Ariana recognized all too well and which caused her to warn, "You're not to interfere, Gran. There's been enough of that already."

Penelope smiled blandly. "I agree," she surprised Ariana by saying. "And I wouldn't dream of interfering. Pack a bag. You can stay with me at Le Premier until we return home. I'll ask your father to gather up the rest of your belongings here. It's the least he can do given the circumstances."

Ariana didn't argue. She didn't think she had any argument left in her. No emotions. No tears. No hope. She kneaded her palm. No Inferno. Without Lazz, the burn would cool, fading to no more than a memory. Any minute now, it would ease. It had to. She didn't think she could live with the heartache, otherwise.

She headed for her bedroom and, once there, closed the door and sagged against it. Who was she kidding? She'd have to find a way to live with it. Because, no matter how hard she might try and wish The Inferno away, it wasn't going anywhere anytime soon.

Sev opened the door to his Pacific Heights home and stepped back. "I thought you might show up here," he informed Lazz. "Come on in."

"How did you—"

"Penelope called, though I gather it was against your wife's express wishes. She filled me in on what happened between you and Ariana."

Lazz took a moment to digest that. "Did she also tell you Brimstone is gone?"

"No, she told me Brimstone's been found." Sev

chuckled, his eyes turning a rich, dark gold. "Judging by your expression, I gather that's news to you. Come on. I think you could use a drink."

"Explain first," Lazz ordered.

"Okay, Mr. Logic. See if you can follow this." Sev led the way to his study while he gave his brother the short-hand version of what Penelope had done with the diamond and how Ariana had unwittingly disposed of it.

When Sev finished, Lazz held out his hand. "Give me that drink," he ordered. He snatched the tumbler from Sev and tossed back the generous finger of whiskey in a single swallow. "Well, hell."

"I'd say that pretty much sums it up," Sev concurred. "Which leaves us with a choice. We can go after the diamond, assuming it hasn't already been passed along. Or we can let it go and allow fate to control its destiny."

Lazz grimaced. "If my vote counts for anything, I say let it go. That damn rock has been nothing but bad luck since the day it was ripped from the ground." He fixed his brother with a wary eye. "You've done a fan-tastic job of returning Dantes to its former position in the jewelry world. We don't need Brimstone to solidify our financial or business position, do we?"

"No, we don't. And it may interest you to know that your vote makes it unanimous."

Lazz couldn't conceal his surprise. "You discussed this with Nicolò and Marco?"

"I just got off the phone with them. If you choose not to try and recover the diamond, the rest of us will go along with your decision."

No question. No hesitation. "Let it go. If the Romanos want to track it down, let them. But my opinion is that no one should benefit from that rock."

After helping himself to a drink and refreshing Lazz's, Sev settled on the couch and waved his brother toward a nearby chair. "Next order of business. Now that all the secrets are out in the open, what do you plan to do about Ariana?"

"What we agreed from the beginning. End the marriage."

Compassion tarnished Sev's gaze. "She made a mistake, Lazz."

"She betrayed me."

"She was protecting her family. No doubt it's been drummed into her the same way it's been drummed into us. That doesn't mean she's not your soul mate. That doesn't mean you didn't experience The Inferno with her."

"Don't."

"You still don't believe, do you?" Sev leaned forward and rested his forearms on his knees. "Why, Lazz? You're the most logical of us all. How can you deny its existence when the evidence is all around you?"

"You're forgetting one vital piece of that evidence." Lazz's mouth compressed. "You're forgetting that Dad and I share similar personalities. You're forgetting that The Inferno didn't work for him and Mom."

Sev tilted his head back and swore. "Of course. I am *such* an idiot. I had no idea you thought that or I'd have set you straight years ago. But you were only a teenager when our parents died, and I didn't want to destroy your memories of them." He released his breath in a sigh. "Dad absolutely believed in The Inferno. But he and Mom never felt it toward each other."

Lazz froze. *"What?"*

"After they died, I found letters indicating that Dad had experienced The Inferno with one of his designers. He chose to ignore what he felt, despite Primo's warnings. He married Mom for her business contacts…and regretted it for the rest of his life. That's why he drafted that contract with Vittorio. He saw an incipient form of The Inferno spark when you and Ariana first touched as children, and he wanted to be certain that the son who most shared his logical bent wouldn't make the same mistake he made."

"How do you know this?"

"From the letters. And I've spoken to Primo and Vittorio about it." Sev paused. "And because you're sitting there attempting to rub a hole in your palm."

Silence reigned for five solid minutes before Lazz spoke again. "I don't know if I can let go," he confessed. "I don't know if I can choose the possibility over the reality."

Sev took a second to gather his arguments. "I understand what you're going through. So do Marco and Nicolò, since we've all been there. We've sat right where you're sitting now and faced the same decision. You have two choices, Lazz. You can forgive your wife, surrender to The Inferno and have a life fuller and richer than you can possibly imagine. Or you can make the same mistake our father made and die in perpetual regret. I suggest you choose fast, before it's too late." He stood. "Now get the hell out of here before I beat your decision into that ugly mug of yours."

Lazz had no memory of returning to his apartment. When he opened the door, he could feel the lack of connection, the sense of emptiness that signaled his wife's absence. Even so, he called to her, praying she'd respond with an enthusiastic volley of Italian. Of course, there was no answer. But there was a message from Vittorio.

I've collected all of Ariana's belongings except her paintings. Will return later tonight for those.

At a loss, Lazz wandered through the empty apartment. He couldn't help but notice that the bits and pieces that Ariana had contributed to his home—and his life—had been stripped away, leaving it cold and sterile. He fought against a pain he had no hope of easing. Had he really lived like this before Ariana? How the hell had he survived it?

Eventually, he found himself in the Mrs. Pennywinkle room. He glanced around, absorbing the beauty and whimsy of his wife's artwork. It was a beauty and whimsy that had slipped into the other areas of his apartment and into all aspects of his life. Into his heart and mind and body. And straight into his soul.

Sev was right. He could reject it, reject The Inferno, along with his wife. Or he could embrace the true meaning of the legend. He could embrace the love that Ariana had given him so unstintingly. The joy and laughter and passion. And he could give it back to her just as unstintingly. He could have love, or he could cling to his common sense and reason and return to the barren existence he'd known before.

It didn't take any thought at all.

He bent down and picked up a piece of paper that had missed the trash can, realizing as he started to ball it up that it was a letter. Aaron Talbot's name leapt off the page and Lazz stiffened as he read. Son of a— He pulled out his cell phone and punched in Penelope's number. She answered on the first ring.

"Talbot rejected Ariana?" he asked tersely.

"Yes," she confirmed. "Ever since Aaron took control of his father's publishing firm, he's been fanatical about preserving the sanctity of Mrs. Pennywinkle. Young fool. At least Jonah would have been more open to change."

"I can fix this," he offered. "I just need time."

There was a brief pause. "What's the point, since Ariana's returning to Italy? Your marriage is over, isn't it? Isn't that what you told her?"

He didn't hesitate. "Not by a long shot."

"It took you long enough to come to your senses," she said with a touch of acid. "Now, what are you going to do to straighten out this mess?"

He grinned as he glanced around the room at his wife's paintings. His gaze narrowed as an idea came to him. Maybe. Just maybe… "First, I need you to delay Ariana for a day or two," he said. "Assuming you're willing."

"I could be talked into it," she graciously conceded.

"Next, I'm going to get my digital camera and take a few pictures. And then you're going to tell me how to get in touch with Aaron's father."

"Ma'am?" The bellboy hovered by the open door to the hotel room. "Your grandmother is waiting in the limousine. She asked if you'd come now."

Ariana gathered up her handbag and gave the suite a final check. "I'm ready."

Lazz stepped into the room. "Actually, she's not.

Tell the limo driver he can leave now. I'll escort Mrs. Dante to the airport."

It took Ariana an instant to react, just long enough for Lazz to hand the bellboy a bill and jerk his head toward the door. With a cheeky grin, the boy snagged the Do Not Disturb sign and hung it on the outside handle before closing the door behind him.

"You can't do that," she protested. "I have a plane to catch."

He crossed to the sitting area and dropped his briefcase onto the coffee table. "There will be other flights if you miss this one. But there might not be another opportunity for us."

She wanted to resist. Wanted to turn and run before he hurt her again. But something kept her from leaving. Maybe it was the sincerity in his eyes and voice. Or maybe it was something else. Something that caused a fragile seedling of hope to blossom with new life. "Okay, I'm listening."

He opened the briefcase he carried and pulled out a sheaf of papers. "I assume you recognize this."

"Is that the contract our parents signed?"

He nodded. "As well as the list of conditions we agreed to."

"That's why you've come?" she demanded, outraged. "You're going to throw those in my face? Try and bind me to you with a pile of documents that never should have been drafted in the first place? You think you're going to keep me here with rules and logic and paper?"

"Not even a little." In one swift motion, he ripped the papers in half and tossed them to the carpet in a flurry of black and white. "I'm hoping to keep you here because of a marriage. Our marriage."

The seedling that had taken root unfurled, its roots grappling to anchor into good, strong soil, while its leaves reached toward the warmth of the sun, toward an Inferno of light and heat. "Go on." She couldn't contain the smile flirting with her mouth. "I'm back to listening."

He reached into his briefcase again and pulled out more papers that reeked of "contract." "And then there's this," he said.

She was tempted to follow his example and rip those apart, as well. "What is it with you Dantes and contracts?" she muttered.

"I think this is one contract you're going to like. It's for a new Mrs. Pennywinkle book." He held it out. "It's yours, if you want it. All you have to do is sign."

She shook her head, stunned. "I don't understand. Aaron rejected me as my grandmother's replacement. How did you manage this, Lazz? What have you done?" Her eyes widened in dismay. "Tell me you didn't bribe him."

He chuckled, the sound deep and rich, causing tendrils of desire to slip through her and grab hold. "I didn't bribe him with anything more than your own artwork."

"How?"

He removed the mock-up of the book he'd created and handed it her. "With this."

She took it from him and flipped through it. Tears filled her eyes. "You made this and showed it to Aaron? It must have taken you forever to put together."

"It didn't take forever. Just a very long twenty-four hours."

It took her a moment before she could speak through her tears. "And it convinced Aaron to give me a contract?"

"There might have been a tiny bit of prodding from Aaron's father. But you got the contract through your own hard work and talent. Your illustrations sold you, not me. They just needed to see the evidence in a more recognizable form. And now that they have they've realized what I did from the start. You, Mrs. Pennywinkle, are amazing." He took the book from her and set it aside. Then he gathered her close. He ran his thumbs along her cheekbones, brushing away the tears. "Does this give you enough reason to stay in San Francisco, instead of returning to Italy?"

She shook her head. "I can be Mrs. Pennywinkle in Italy just as easily as here," she pointed out. "If you want me to stay, give me a better reason."

"I thought you might say that. And my response is…" His voice altered, softened. The words were filled with unwavering certainty and a passion she couldn't mistake. "Stay because of me. Because of us. Not because of a diamond, or a contract or family obligations. Let's start over, for the right reasons this time."

"And what reasons are those?"

He didn't hesitate. "Because we belong together. We have from the very first touch. My world exploded around me that day and it's never been the same since."

"Exploded?"

The expression that swept across his face dazzled her. "Burst into flames?" he dared to tease.

She stilled. "Are you telling me you believe in The Inferno now?"

"I believe in this…" He threaded his fingers through hers until their palms met and the warmth came. "If this is The Inferno, then yes. I believe in The Inferno."

It took her a moment to gather herself enough to respond. "Even though it defies logic and common sense?" she managed to ask.

His smile turned tender. "I sacrificed those the moment we first joined hands. And I would much rather have what I found as a replacement."

"And what's that?" she whispered, daring to hope. Daring to believe.

"Love. I love you, Ariana Dante."

It was all she wanted him to say and everything she needed to hear. "And I love you."

Her arms tightened around his neck and she kissed him. Kissed him until the fires burned and they were consumed in the flames. He swept her into his arms and carried her to the bed. He lowered her into a nest of down and butter-soft cotton, his weight a delicious dichotomy to the smoothness beneath her.

He feathered a kiss across her lips, just a quiet, fleeting pressure that still managed to push her ever closer to that delicious edge between reason and insanity. Between need and desperation.

"I can't imagine my life without you," he admitted between kisses.

"But if I'd left…"

He smoothed her hair back from her face. "I'd have come after you. You are…" He lowered his head, burying his face in the crook of her shoulder. He inhaled her scent before pressing a string of kisses along the length of her neck. Then he found her mouth again, his hunger for her taking on a sharp edge. "You are everything to me. You are my life."

"Oh, Lazz." She cupped his face. "Haven't you figured it out yet? Don't you realize that it's the same for me?"

"I'd hoped," he admitted gruffly.

They moved in concert, their clothing slipping away in a slow, sweet process interrupted by kisses and filled with intimate laughter. When nothing remained between them, she reached for him, surprised when he stopped her at the last moment.

"I didn't come prepared. Is it safe to make love?" he asked.

"Not even a little," she warned.

Satisfaction swept across his face. "I was hoping you'd say that. Do you mind?"

She didn't hesitate. "Not even a little," she repeated softly.

They didn't speak again for a long, long time. This time when they came together it was different. It was as if those other occasions had been mere shadows of the real thing. Preludes to a song as yet unsung. As though they'd experienced only the disparate parts without ever knowing the whole. This time all the pieces came together, locking into place and creating a union of intense color and light and rightness. This time they surrendered everything they had, giving themselves up to love.

And in that ultimate joining, the Inferno had fulfilled its promise. The last Dante man fell. In fact, the last Dante man didn't just fall into the flames.

He leapt.

*   *   *   *   *

Here's a sneak peek at
THE CEO'S CHRISTMAS PROPOSITION,
the first in USA TODAY *bestselling author*
Merline Lovelace's *HOLIDAYS ABROAD trilogy*
coming in November 2008.

American Devon McShay is about to get the
Christmas surprise of a lifetime when she meets
her new client, sexy billionaire Caleb Logan, for
the very first time.

Silhouette
Desire

Available November 2008

Her breath whistled out in a sigh of relief when he exited Customs. Devon recognized him right away from the newspaper and magazine articles her friend and partner Sabrina had looked up during her frantic prep work.

Caleb John Logan, Jr. Thirty-one. Six-two. With jet-black hair, laser-blue eyes and a linebacker's shoulders under his charcoal-gray cashmere overcoat. His jaw-dropping good looks didn't score him any points with Devon. She'd learned the hard way not to trust handsome heartbreakers like Cal Logan.

But he was a client. An important one. And she was willing to give someone who'd served a hitch in the marines before earning a B.S. from the University of Oregon, an MBA from Stanford and his first million at the ripe old age of twenty-six the benefit of the doubt.

Right up until he spotted the hot-pink pashmina, that is.

Devon knew the flash of color was more visible than the sign she held up with his name on it. So she wasn't surprised when Logan picked her out of the crowd and cut in her direction. She'd just plastered on her best businesswoman smile when he whipped an arm around her waist. The next moment she was sprawled against his cashmere-covered chest.

"Hello, brown eyes."

Swooping down, he covered her mouth with his.

Sheer astonishment kept Devon rooted to the spot for a few seconds while her mind whirled chaotically. Her first thought was that her client had downed a few too many drinks during the long flight. Her second, that he'd mistaken the kind of escort and consulting services her company provided. Her third shoved everything else out of her head.

The man could kiss!

His mouth moved over hers with a skill that ignited sparks at a half dozen flash points throughout her body. Devon hadn't experienced that kind of spontaneous combustion in a while. A *long* while.

The sparks were still popping when she pushed off his chest, only now they fueled a flush of anger.

"Do you always greet women you don't know with a lip-lock, Mr. Logan?"

A smile crinkled the skin at the corners of his eyes. "As a matter of fact, I don't. That was from Don."

"Huh?"

"He said he owed you one from New Year's Eve two years ago and made me promise to deliver it."

She stared up at him in total incomprehension. Logan hooked a brow and attempted to prompt a non-existent memory.

"He abandoned you at the Waldorf. Five minutes before midnight. To deliver twins."

"I don't have a clue who or what you're…"

Understanding burst like a water balloon.

"Wait a sec. Are you talking about Sabrina's old boyfriend? Your buddy, who's now an ob-gyn doc?"

It was Logan's turn to look startled. He recovered faster than Devon had, though. His smile widened into a rueful grin.

"I take it you're not Sabrina Russo."

"No, Mr. Logan, I am *not*."

* * * * *

Be sure to look for
THE CEO'S CHRISTMAS PROPOSITION
by Merline Lovelace.
Available in November 2008 wherever books are sold, including most bookstores, supermarkets, drugstores and discount stores.

REQUEST YOUR FREE BOOKS!

2 FREE NOVELS PLUS 2 FREE GIFTS!

Silhouette® Desire®

Passionate, Powerful, Provocative!

MARRIED BY CHRISTMAS

Playboy billionaire Elijah Vanaldi has discovered
he is guardian to his small orphaned nephew.
But his reputation makes some people question
his ability to be a father. He knows he must
fight to protect the child, and he'll do anything
it takes. Ainslie Farrell is jobless, homeless and
desperate—and when Elijah offers her a position
in his household she simply can't refuse....

Available in November

HIRED: THE ITALIAN'S CONVENIENT MISTRESS
by
CAROL MARINELLI
Book #29

nocturne™

ESCAPE THE CHILL OF WINTER WITH TWO SPECIAL STORIES FROM BESTSELLING AUTHORS

MICHELE HAUF

AND

VIVI ANNA

WINTER KISSED

In "A Kiss of Frost," photographer Kate Wilson experiences the icy kisses of Jal Frosti, but soon learns that this icy god has a deadly ulterior motive. Can Kate's love melt his heart?

In "Ice Bound," Dr. Darien Calder travels to the north island of Japan, where he discovers an icy goddess who is rumored to freeze doomed travelers. Darien is determined to melt her beautiful but frosty exterior and break her of the curse she carries...before it's too late.

Available November wherever books are sold.

Silhouette®

Romantic
SUSPENSE

**Sparked by Danger,
Fueled by Passion.**

Lindsay McKenna
Susan Grant

Mission: Christmas

Celebrate the holidays with a pair
of military heroines and their daring men
in two romantic, adventurous stories
from these bestselling authors.

Featuring:

"The Christmas Wild Bunch"
by *USA TODAY* bestselling author
Lindsay McKenna

and

"Snowbound with a Prince"
by *New York Times* bestselling author
Susan Grant

Available November wherever books are sold.

COMING NEXT MONTH

#1903 PREGNANT ON THE UPPER EAST SIDE?—
Emilie Rose
Park Avenue Scandals
This powerful Manhattan attorney uses a business proposal to seduce his beautiful party planner into bed. After their one night of passion, could she be carrying his baby?

#1904 THE MAGNATE'S TAKEOVER—Mary McBride
Gifts from a Billionaire
When they first met, he didn't tell her he was the enemy. But as they grow ever closer, he risks revealing his true identity and motives, and destroying everything.

#1905 THE CEO'S CHRISTMAS PROPOSITION—
Merline Lovelace
Holidays Abroad
Stranded in Austria together at Christmas, it only takes one kiss for him to decide he wants more than just a business relationship. And this CEO always gets what he wants....

#1906 DO NOT DISTURB UNTIL CHRISTMAS—
Charlene Sands
Suite Secrets
Reunited with his ex-love, he plans to leave her first this time—until he discovers she's pregnant! Will their marriage of convenience bring him a change of heart?

#1907 SPANIARD'S SEDUCTION—Tessa Radley
The Saxon Brides
A mysterious stranger shows up with a secret and a heart set on revenge. Then he meets the one woman whose love could change all his plans.

#1908 BABY BEQUEST—Robyn Grady
Billionaires and Babies
He proposed a temporary marriage to help her get custody of her orphaned niece, but their passion was all too permanent.

SDCNMBPA1008